The Night After Tomorrow

January . . . the wolf month . . . wolf-monath . . .

Jess felt she had been broken to pieces. Nothing worked for her any more. So it was good to get away and find some space with her aunt in the country.

But the country wasn't quite as peaceful as she thought it would be. In the forest there were strange noises and movements. When Jess was in bed, there was the sense of someone or something outside, watching, waiting for her. On the farms, the cattle and sheep were being slaughtered by a savage creature — the forest beast they called it.

And then there was Luc, who seemed to belong to the wild, with his hypnotic amber-coloured eyes and long hair. Why was he so interested in the forest beast? Why had no one ever seen his mother? And what was it that could only be done the night after tomorrow?

Sue Welford was born in Sussex and trained to be a secretary before giving up work to bring up her children. When they started school, she had several part-time jobs, and then became an editorial writer with a local newspaper. When she was made redundant, she continued writing at home and had several articles published in magazines. After five rejected novels, her first book for young adults was published in 1989. *The Night After Tomorrow* is the fourth of her books to be published by Oxford University Press.

Charlie In The Pink
ISBN 0 19 271698 0

'a funny home-and-school story with a trendy theme: Mum is a green feminist; step-dad is a New Man.' *The Economist*

Ghost In The Mirror
ISBN 0 19 271704 9

'a spicy mixture of mystery, everyday grittiness, and romance.' *Sunday Times*

Snowbird Winter
ISBN 0 19 271729 4

'They saw a strange, boiling whirlpool of mist. Gradually, from its centre, a shape emerged. Shadowy. Almost transparent. On wings the colour of moonlight, it flew towards them. Instinctively, as the bird flew overhead, they both ducked, then turned, their eyes tracking the creature as it flew downriver. The shape disappeared into the gloom. They stood watching, waiting . . .'

The Night After Tomorrow

The Night After Tomorrow

Sue Welford

Oxford University Press
Oxford New York Toronto

Oxford University Press, Walton Street, Oxford OX2 6DP

Oxford New York Toronto
Delhi Bombay Calcutta Madras Karachi
Kuala Lumpur Singapore Hong Kong Tokyo
Nairobi Dar es Salaam Cape Town
Melbourne Auckland Madrid

and associated companies in
Berlin Ibadan

Oxford is a trade mark of Oxford University Press

Copyright © Sue Welford 1995
First published 1995

ISBN 0 19 271726 X

A CIP catalogue record for this book is available
from the British Library

Printed and bound in Great Britain by
Biddles Ltd, Guildford and King's Lynn

1

JESS

There was someone else in the forest. Jess knew as soon as she stepped inside. There was no sound. Only the far distant roar of a low-flying jet abused the silence. Still, she knew someone was there. A scalpel of terror slid into the back of her neck. She turned sharply but there was no one to be seen. Only a fleeting, golden shadow of movement that hovered on the edge of reality then was gone.

Jess had walked to the village to get a newspaper. The headline leapt out at her. *'Forest Beast Strikes Again.'* The smaller headline—*'Prize cattle slaughtered in frenzied attack.'* Her stomach churned, shock numbed her scalp. Unwillingly, her eyes scanned the next few lines. *'In the latest of a series of mysterious attacks on livestock, farmer John Boughton of Lower Ridge . . .'*

Jess couldn't read any more. The picture of the cow with its throat slashed, half its back leg torn off, was more than she could bear. She had always hated that kind of thing . . . the thought of animals being hunted and killed. She could never bear those wildlife programmes that showed lions attacking gazelles, dogs tearing a rabbit to pieces . . . they always made her want to cry.

With a shudder Jess wrenched her eyes away from the headline. She left the paper in the rack.

Jess stood with her back against the trunk of a huge oak tree. She put her arms behind her, round the trunk as far as they

1

would go. She pressed her spine against the hard, knobbly bark. It gave strange comfort, a feeling of solidarity. As if she was real after all. Not just a mourning shadow of a girl who had once been happy. The tree had been here for a hundred years, maybe more. Jess leaned her head, looking up at the labyrinth of branches against a leaden sky.

Jess suddenly felt hungry. It must be the long walk . . . the fresh, forest air. Jess couldn't remember the last time she had enjoyed food. She raised a hand to brush away a lock of hair. Her fingers were long and slender, clawlike. Like a bird's hands, her friend Emma said. It was funny when you lost weight. Everything got smaller. Not just hips, thighs. Your shoes got too big, rings slid about on your fingers, your watch fell round the wrong way. Relatives used to say Jess looked like her grandmother as a young girl. Pale, freckled skin, chestnut hair, curls highlighting red in the sun . . . a round face. When Jess looked in the mirror now there were high cheekbones she didn't know she had. There were pools of sadness beneath green eyes . . .

As usual, Danny came into her thoughts. Being in the forest reminded her of that day in the park . . . under the tree . . . the day he first told her he loved her . . . that she was the only one.

Jess wiped away an angry tear.

She started to run. She still felt convinced there was someone there . . . hiding in the trees . . . watching, waiting . . .

The wind, swishing through the branches, seemed to be saying her name.

Jess . . . Jess . . .

It felt good to run. It stopped her brooding. Her trainers sent a scattering of leaves behind her. She could hear her breath coming out in gasps. The cold air sent sharp knives into her lungs. She stopped again, skidding into a dune of leaves piled against a bank. She glanced behind, then took a deep breath. Held it . . . She ran on again, towards the clearing.

Towards the figure she somehow knew was there . . .

Waiting . . .

The forest was cool, quiet. A weak shaft of sunlight shimmered on the bronze carpet of leaves. Jess slowed to a trot, a walk. She put her arms round herself and hugged. Whoever it was . . . the *someone* was giving her the creeps. They seemed to be pulling her on invisible threads. Why didn't she go back the other way? It would take a bit longer but what did it matter? Jess had all the time in the world. She could run along the bridle path, across the common to the road. People. Safety. It would be no use calling for help so deep in the forest. There was no one to hear . . . only the trees. Nothing but time and space . . . no one . . . no one except . . .

'It'll do you good to get away,' her mother had said before she left. 'There's too much here that reminds you of Danny. A few weeks with your Aunt Peggy and you'll be dying to come home.'

Or would she just be dying?

Jess knew her parents had despaired of her ever getting back to normal. Six months of mourning, they said, was long enough. Six months . . . ? Jess knew she would never get over what had happened . . . six months, six years . . . six times for ever.

Her father had only made a token protest about her going away, missing the beginning of the new college term. He had been content, as always, to let Jess's mother make the decisions. Just so long as he was left in peace and quiet with his music after his hard days at the office.

He hadn't even said much to Jess when Danny died. He had just mumbled 'I'm sorry' when he saw his daughter broken to pieces, scattered like the remains of Danny's smashed motor bike. Jess supposed her father might even be relieved. She knew he didn't like Danny. All the signs were there . . . the frown of annoyance when she got in late; the suggestion that if she 'got tangled up' with anyone it might interfere with her education. Especially someone like Danny. It was as if anyone who wore a leather jacket and rode a motor bike represented all that was wrong with the world. Her father had even tried to stop her seeing him . . . sending out messages of disapproval through Jess's mother.

It hadn't worked.

Nothing worked.

Not any more.

Jess looked up. She frowned, catching the shadow of movement. A four-footed flash of bronze . . . an eddy of leaves. A pheasant, startled, flapping, fleeting in terror. A feather falling from its dappled tail. As if a hand had tried to grab it as it flew. The headline burned again.

'*Prize cattle killed in* . . .'

If Jess's mother had been there she'd have warned her. '*Don't come back through the forest . . . Little Red Riding Hood . . . It's too dangerous. There could be . . . things . . . people . . . lurking about.*'

But her aunt didn't say things like that. She wasn't like other people. Peggy believed you should be free to make your own decisions.

'I don't know how two sisters could be so different,' Jess had heard her father say to her mother over the breakfast table one morning. As usual, Jess had cried off breakfast, saying she wasn't hungry. Her mother's tight, white lips had been a mark of her silent disapproval. Jess had heard the conversation from the front room where she had been sitting, staring at the blank television screen, thinking, as usual, about Danny.

'Brought up in the same environment . . . ' her father's voice had drifted into her consciousness. 'It just doesn't fit in with any of the psychological theories.'

4

Jess's father was always on about psychological theories, trying to fit people into the little compartments made for them by various ancient professors who had merely done experiments with baby monkeys and bundles of cloth or hysterical Victorian women.

'We're just different by nature,' Jess's mother had insisted. 'I'm gregarious, Peggy's a loner . . . simple as that.'

'Yes, but living in that place . . . miles from anywhere. It's not natural.'

Jess really didn't know how her father knew what was natural and what wasn't. Living in his own artificial world of profits and computers and stereo systems and golf on Sundays. How on earth would he know?

'But it will do Jess good to get away,' her mother had insisted. Jess had heard the desperation in her voice. 'We've done all we can. And Peggy is her godmother after all.'

Jess had heard her father sigh. 'Well, OK, if you say so, Ruth, but I really don't see what good it will do.'

Jess hadn't been able to stand any more. She had stormed into the room.

'Stop talking about me!' she shouted. 'If you've got anything to say, say it to my face!'

Her parents had glanced at her, shocked that their innocent conversation had incited such anger in the daughter they thought they knew.

'Your father was only saying he didn't think going to Peggy's would do you much good,' her mother explained.

'I know. I heard.' Jess had looked at her father with tears in her eyes. 'I just want to get away, Dad . . . I *need* space.' Jess couldn't imagine why she felt the obligation to explain.

Her father had looked away, embarrassed as usual by any display of emotion. He shrugged. 'OK, Jess. I suppose if you're miserable you can always come home. You only have to ring.'

Jess had put her hand on her father's arm. 'I'm miserable here, Dad.'

He had glanced at her, puzzled. He didn't understand. He had never understood. 'Yes . . . I know,' he mumbled. 'I'm concerned about college, that's all.'

Jess shrugged. 'Mum's right, I'll soon catch up. I won't be miserable, you know I love it there.'

Jess had thought about the time she stayed with Peggy before. She had only been ten. Her mother had gone with her then . . . she had hated it . . . couldn't wait to get home. But Jess had loved Peggy's big, rambling house on the edge of the forest. She had adored helping with the animals, walking the dogs. Anyway, she didn't care about college . . . about anything. All she cared about was that Danny was dead and she couldn't forget him.

Her father had put his computer magazine away in his brief-case. 'If you flunk your first year it'll lessen your chances of going to university.' He had shrugged. 'Still, it's your life . . . '

Or my death . . .

Jess had wanted to say she didn't care about stupid college, or stupid university. But even then she couldn't hurt her father that way. She knew he harboured for her all the dreamt of opportunities he had missed himself.

She had bitten her lip. Hard. As if a new pain might take the old one away.

The boy was sitting on a fallen tree trunk a few metres in front of her. His face was lifted, nostrils flared, sniffing the wind. As if the scent of her loneliness had reached him in advance.

She stood between two slender birch trees at the edge of the clearing. Looking.

So this was the *someone* she'd known was here. Her foot cracked a twig.

He turned, the breeze stirring the hair on the back of his head like a dog's hackles rising. He seemed scared, ready for flight. His eyes narrowed as she stood there.

It should be me who's scared. Meeting a stranger in the middle of a forest. I should run . . . who knows what could . . . what big teeth you have Grand—
Had she been crazy to walk there alone?

She was snared by his gaze, his beauty. His eyes were bright, full of shifting spiral shadows and topaz light. He had deep golden, shoulder-length hair. His gaze caught and held her. She knew they saw her despair. She shivered as if someone had walked over Danny's grave.

The boy frowned and went on staring. He wore scruffy jeans, a tan leather jacket, zipped to the top. Jess thought for one minute he was going to say something.

She raised her hand but he was gone. Jumping to his feet, running silently into the trees. His figure merged with the shadows like a departing ghost.

'Wait . . . !'

His flight had breached the dam of her tears.

Jess sat on the tree trunk and wept.

'That would be the boy from Gollum Castle.'

Gollum, the creepy, slimy ring-stealer from *Lord of the Rings*.

'Gollum Castle? You're joking!' Jess exclaimed.

Peggy laughed. 'That's not its real name. Just what I call it.' She filled two buckets with water. Jess followed, dragging the bale of straw towards the donkey shelter. 'It looks like the place where someone like Gollum should live,' she added.

'What's its real name then?'

'I don't know,' Peggy grunted as she lifted the buckets to fill the trough. 'Here . . .' she handed Jess a knife. Jess cut the twine and spread the straw on the floor of the shelter, blowing now and then on her frozen fingers. 'It's that old place on the north edge of the forest,' Peggy explained. 'You pass it on the way to the main road. You can just see it in the winter when the trees are bare. It's got a wall round it but you can still see the garden's like a jungle. It's always looked like a castle to me. They only use one wing now apparently. Most of the rest is derelict.'

'How do you know?'

'It's common knowledge. The family have lived there for years.'

'Family?'

'Well . . . the boy and his mother. They're the only ones left now. They're of French descent but they've lived in England for several generations. There's a story that—'

'What?'

Peggy shrugged. 'Oh, nothing, it's only village gossip . . . you know I hate that kind of thing.'

But Jess wouldn't let it go.

'Oh, tell me, Peggy,' she begged.

Peggy strode through the gate. She kicked it shut with her muddy wellington boot. She put the buckets down and tied the gate up with baler twine. 'People say the family escaped from persecution in France, that's all.'

'What—you mean some kind of religious persecution?'

'Something like that. No one really knows. And they never mix with anyone . . . the boy didn't even go to school.'

Jess frowned. 'Didn't go to school? That's strange.'

'You can teach kids at home if you get permission from the authorities. I suppose that's what his mother did . . . maybe still does . . . he's only about your age, I should think.'

'Have you ever seen him in the forest, then?'

Peggy shook her head. 'No, I've seen him shopping in the village a few times. And he came here once.'

'Here? What for?'

They crossed the frozen yard. The buckets clashed together as Peggy put them inside the store. She blew through the holes in her tatty, woollen gloves. 'Come on, let's get inside. My fingers are falling off. I'll tell you the rest of the story indoors.'

Jess sat by the range in the untidy Victorian kitchen. Amongst an assortment of jugs and cups, postcards and photographs on the old dresser was a row of home-made jams and pickles. Above, Peggy had hung bunches of lavender and herbs to dry. Their smell reminded Jess of summer. She clasped a mug of hot Bovril. The warmth gradually seeped through her fingers. Her other hand caressed the tabby cat, purring on her lap. She felt the rumbling, deep in its body like the stirring of an earthquake.

There was something aromatic bubbling on the stove.

'I made some soup if you fancy it,' Peggy said. 'Mushroom, I picked them myself at the end of the summer and dried them in the airing cupboard. They make good soup with a few herbs and potatoes.'

'Great, thanks,' Jess still felt hungry.

Peggy looked at her with raised eyebrows. It must be the first time since arriving that Jess had actually wanted to eat. Peggy never tried to force her. The food was there, she helped herself if she fancied anything.

Jess looked up. Peggy sat opposite in an old wooden rocking-chair. She stretched her toes towards the fire. Her huge fisherman's socks had holes in. Beneath, she wore another pair, striped, hand-knitted from the homespun wool of her Jacob sheep.

'Tell me more about that boy,' Jess said, her curiosity aroused by Peggy's tales of gothic castles and rampant gardens. 'Why did he come here?'

'I had a Canadian timber wolf. He came to see it,' Peggy explained. 'The wolf was beautiful. He'd been loose in the forest for some time. He'd escaped from a private collection. Jack managed to tranquillize him . . . '

'Jack?'

'Jack Stride, the vet.'

'Oh . . . ' Jess wasn't sure but she thought Peggy flushed at the mention of Jack Stride's name.

'I've got a picture somewhere . . . of the wolf, I mean,' Peggy said with a grin.

9

She tipped a black kitten off her knees and moved aside a pile of yellowed newspapers from the front of the cupboard. More fell out when she opened the door. After Jess's mother's obsessive tidiness, being here was like being in heaven.

Peggy dragged out a brown envelope and tipped its contents out on the floor. Jess grinned to herself. The thought of her mother's face if such a thing happened at home filled her with an impulse to laugh out loud.

Peggy scrabbled around, frowning to see in the dim light. Her hair fell in front of her face and she pushed it back.

'Christ,' she said impatiently, looking upward, 'this light's abysmal.'

Jess didn't like to suggest she got a stronger bulb.

'God!' Peggy picked out a photograph of a man standing by a boat. She handed it to Jess with a wry grin. 'My husband . . . the one who should have put me off men for life.'

The man was wearing shorts and nothing else.

'What was he like?'

'A pig. Good looking though, don't you think?'

'Yes.' His dark hair, his tanned skin, reminded Jess of Danny. Her heart turned over.

'They're the bloody worst. If you're knocked out by their looks, then you can bet your sweet life all the other women are as well.'

'Yes.' Jess handed the picture back. 'Why did you leave him?'

'Didn't your mother tell you?'

Jess shook her head. 'No.'

Peggy stared at the photo. 'He was a bastard. He knocked me about. I put up with it for five years . . . '

'You must have been nuts. I'm blowed if I'd stay with someone that long.'

Peggy shrugged. 'I must have been. Although women do, you see . . . some put up with bastards all their lives.'

Jess examined her thumb nail. 'They love them, I suppose. Whatever they do to them.'

'Yes, and they keep thinking each time will be the last.' She looked at Jess. 'And they're so sorry, you see, Jess, every time they do it, they're so sorry afterwards. It's crazy but you keep on forgiving them until one day you just snap.'

'I can believe it. There's other kinds of cruelty too, isn't there?'

Peggy looked at Jess shrewdly. 'Yes, lots . . . '

'Like telling lies and pretending to be something you're not.'

'Yes,' said Peggy. She looked as if she was waiting for Jess to go on.

Jess pointed to the pile of photographs. 'You were looking for a picture of the wolf, remember?'

'Oh . . . oh, yes. Ah . . . here it is.' Peggy held up another picture. 'Knew it was here somewhere.' She tucked a strand of straggly fair hair behind one ear. A smile crossed her sharp features. 'I called him Sleet. Fatal that, giving them names. It's as if they become yours if you name them. You never want to let them go.' Peggy held the picture towards the light, squinting. 'You know, Jess, there were lots of native American wolf tribes and clans. Some tribes even believed they were descended from wolves.'

Jess took the photograph. The wolf had small, golden eyes, a pale, grey-flecked coat, stippled and sharp-edged in the sunlight.

Jess drew in her breath. 'He's beautiful . . . gorgeous . . . ' There was something about the creature's eyes that seemed to hypnotize her. She looked up ' . . . and that boy came to see him?'

Peggy shoved the photos back into the cupboard, slamming the door quickly before they fell out again. She tucked each hand into opposite sleeves of her baggy jumper, hugging her arms into her waist. She came back to the fire.

'Yes . . . ' she frowned, remembering. 'It was odd, he just appeared one day . . . asked if he could see Sleet. I don't know how he even knew the wolf was here. I kept him in

11

that big outside kennel with the run. The boy just stood at the wire, staring.'

'What happened?'

'Sleet just stared back. Then he came towards him, crawled almost on his belly . . . submissive . . . you know, then he lay on his back with his legs in the air.' Peggy shook her head, 'Odd . . . very odd. In spite of all the legends, wolves are very shy creatures. Sleet usually ran inside if anyone came near. He had been free for some time and didn't trust humans an inch. I'd forgotten about him and the boy. I remember now how strange he was, very shy and childlike, even though he must have been fifteen or sixteen. Where did you say you saw him?'

'In a clearing in the forest.'

'Did he speak to you?'

Jess shook her head. Sadly, although she didn't know why. 'No, he ran away.'

'I don't think he hardly speaks to anyone, he probably has no idea how to communicate properly. I feel sorry for him, living in that old place with just his mother for company. Poor kid. You're right, he is weird, but do you wonder at it?'

'No.' Jess remembered the long hair, the bright-eyed gaze, the frown. As if he had been trying to see inside her head. Her feeling of loss when he ran off . . . she must be going nuts.

Peggy leaned forward to stir the pot on the stove. 'I've lived here for ten years and I've never seen his mother. He does the shopping and everything. She never goes out. No one's seen her for years apparently, although the foresters used to spot her sometimes.'

'What was she doing?'

'Just walking, I think, but she always ran away.'

'I wonder why?'

'She's just odd, I think. The old couple, her parents, didn't mix with the village folk either.'

'What about his father?'

Peggy shrugged. 'No one knows. No one even knew she had a child until the old folk died. It was sad, they both died on the same day. Jack told me the boy ran to the village to summon the doctor.'

'Hasn't anyone ever tried to see them . . . you know, the welfare people?'

'Apparently the doctor tried to go back but the boy's mother wouldn't let her in. She shouted at her through the letter box apparently,' Peggy grinned. 'Swore at her in French.'

'What do they do for money?'

'I suppose they've got family money. They were landowners in France, someone said.' Peggy shrugged. 'I don't know, it's really only gossip. I think the village people are a bit afraid of them, to be honest. You know, old folk tales and superstitions . . . '

Jess's eyes shone. 'Perhaps his mother's mad? Like that woman in *Jane Eyre* . . . what was her name?'

Peggy laughed. 'Umm . . . I've forgotten . . . oh, Bertha or something. Yes, maybe she is.'

'It's not much of a life for the boy. He looked . . .'

'What?'

But *beautiful* was the only word Jess could think of.

Jess stared into the fire. She tried to imagine what it would be like. Living in a ruin, never going outside, never talking to *anyone* except your son.

'They must be terribly lonely,' she said after a while.

'They obviously like it that way. People should be free to live how they choose.'

'Yes,' Jess agreed. 'And there is something about the forest. It gives you a feeling . . . I don't know . . . of security . . . as if you don't ever want to leave.'

'Certainly most people who live near it have done so all their lives. Some of the families go way, way back, generations of forest workers. They wouldn't live anywhere else.'

Jess giggled suddenly. 'I wonder what my dad would think of them . . . the Gollum boy and his mum.'

Peggy smiled. 'I don't know.'

'He thinks anyone who doesn't get their clothes from Marks and Sparks is a hippie. Let alone living like hermits in a castle in the middle of a forest.'

Peggy pulled a face. 'We used to have such good times, your mum and me. I always thought your dad was a bit . . . '

'What?'

'Conventional.'

'You mean boring?'

Peggy smiled. 'Not really boring, just . . . safe. We'd planned so many things.'

'What kind of things?' Jess couldn't imagine her mother planning anything other than what colour to paint the bathroom.

Peggy shrugged. 'Oh . . . we wanted to travel round the world . . . there was this band we were both mad on.'

'Band!' blurted Jess. She just couldn't see her mother as some kind of groupie.

'Yes. They were called Purple Thunder. I suppose today they'd be called heavy metal.'

'Heavy metal!' Jess pretended to roll around the floor with laughter. 'Mum thinks heavy metal is something double-glazing window frames are made of.'

Peggy laughed too. 'Don't you be so cheeky, young lady.'

Jess sobered up. It seemed weird, hearing about her mother as if she really *had* been young once.

'I just can't imagine it, that's all.'

'Why not?'

'Because . . . ' Jess shrugged. 'I don't know . . . '

'Because we grew up?' suggested Peggy with a knowing look in her eye.

'Something like that,' Jess said.

'That's the trouble with being young,' said Peggy wisely. 'You have to grow up.'

'Yes.'

'And some of us give up our dreams and opt for security.'

'Yes. I think that's why my parents worried so much about me and Danny. No job, no security . . . ' she waggled her finger, 'equals "not suitable for our only daughter".'

Peggy must have seen the sudden burst of pain in Jess's eyes.

Everything came round to Danny in the end.

Everything.

Peggy touched her hand lightly. 'Jess, you should talk about Danny more. If you don't, it's as if he never lived.'

Jess looked down at her hands, twisting themselves together in her lap.

'I suppose it's habit,' she said quietly. 'Mum . . . Dad . . . they never wanted to talk about him when he was alive, let alone—'

'They didn't like him much, did they?'

'They didn't know him. How can you not like someone you don't know?'

'Maybe it was just because he was a lot older than you. Your mother told me—'

Jess looked up sharply. 'What? What did she tell you?'

'Nothing really. Just that he was older . . . that he had no job.'

'I suppose they wanted me to fall in love with some boring prat. A bloody Young Conservative or something.'

Peggy grinned. 'It must have been pretty tough for you.'

'It was tough for Danny too. He *wanted* my parents to like him . . . at least . . . '

'What?'

Jess shrugged. 'Oh . . . I don't know.' She shook her head. 'What does it matter now anyway?' She stared into the fire.

'Your grandfather disapproved of my husband too, you know. He tried to stop me marrying him. As it turned out, he was right. Fathers often are.'

Jess looked at her aunt. Peggy's thin face looked sad in

15

the firelight. As if the memory of her quarrels with her father still hurt.

'Not always,' Jess said.

Peggy looked up. 'No . . . not always.'

Jess turned her head away. 'If . . . if my dad had liked Danny . . . if I could have taken him home like other girls take their boyfriends home . . . then Danny wouldn't have had to drop me at the end of the road and that stupid joyrider wouldn't have come shooting round the corner in that XR2—' Her voice broke. She heard it again . . . like an old cassette tape played over and over . . . the screech of brakes, the awful smashing . . . the tinkering of glass . . . the spinning, screaming silence.

'Do you blame him, then?'

'Who, my dad?'

'Yes.'

'Yes . . . ' Jess said bitterly. 'Yes, I do. Danny didn't fit into one of his neat little compartments, so he simply didn't want to know.' She gazed towards the window. She frowned as a shadow darted away.

'He was concerned, Jess, they both were.'

'Yes,' Jess admitted, 'I know . . . '

Silence.

'What happened to your wolf?' Jess asked, suddenly wanting to talk about anything but her parents and Danny.

'Sleet? Oh, he went to a private zoo in Kent. I hated losing him, but wolves are pack animals, they need companionship. They can actually get quite tame. The Eskimos have them. They mate them with their sledge dogs sometimes.'

'They can do that, then? Breed with domestic dogs.'

'Yep, they make brilliant sledge dogs . . . tough, really brave.'

For some reason Jess thought again of the boy in the forest. His topaz glance . . . the question in his eyes.

'Do you know his name by any chance?'

'Who?'

'The forest boy.'

Peggy frowned. She raised her eyes to the ceiling. 'Oh, God. I did know . . . ' She ran her hand over her face. 'No, it's gone . . . I must be going mad. Premature senility's my excuse . . . what's yours?' she joked.

'Premature death,' Jess said. She swallowed. Hard.

Peggy leaned forward once more, fingers cool on Jess's hand. 'You're still feeling sorry for yourself, you know, Jess.'

Jess lowered her lids. She gulped the hard, heavy lump of tears. 'I know. That's why I'm here, isn't it? One last desperate attempt to get rid of my self pity. Thrusting myself on you when everyone else has given up on me.'

Peggy pulled a face. 'Jess?'

Jess felt guilty. None of it was Peggy's fault. Why was she taking it out on her? 'Sorry,' she said.

Peggy leaned forward and took her hand. Jess felt her dry, rough skin, the snagged nails. 'You can talk to me about it any time, Jess. It's the best way to get it out of your system.'

'Yes . . . thanks.'

'Your mum says you've never talked about it . . . about Danny . . . not to her or your dad.'

Jess snorted. 'My dad? You're joking.'

'Well, someone . . . anyone . . . '

'I know. I've wanted to but everyone avoids the subject. Except my friend, Emma. She knew Danny almost as well as I did, or thought she did. Anyway, she hated him . . . she doesn't understand. And people don't want to upset me. They'd be totally embarrassed if I wept in front of them.'

Peggy smiled. 'Well, I don't mind upsetting you. Not if it helps.'

Jess squeezed her hand. 'Thanks, Peggy.'

Peggy stroked the back of Jess's hand absently. 'Would Danny want you to be like this?' she asked.

'Like what?'

'Not eating, hardly sleeping . . . going around in a dream.

Jess, I know you have to mourn, but it's killing you.'

'Well then, tell me what I'm supposed to do? Go around cheering because some stupid kid in a stolen car killed Danny!'

'No,' Peggy said softly. 'Of course not.'

At least she doesn't try to *tell* me what Danny would want, Jess thought. Not like every other stupid twit. How would they know? How would anybody know?

Jess put her hands over her eyes. She took a deep breath, bit down hard on her lip. Stop it! she told herself. Stop!

'I'm sorry,' Jess said. 'I didn't mean . . . '

Peggy was standing in front of her. Her face was saying, I really want to help, what can I do?

Jess reached out. Peggy's hands were still cold. Cold, but oddly comforting. They stood there, hands clasped. Jess wouldn't look. She heaved a shuddering sigh then let go. She shook her head, laughing . . . crying . . .

'I'm OK . . . look . . . '

Peggy laughed with relief. 'That's what you've got to do, Jess. Cry a bloody ocean if you feel like it.'

'Do you think I haven't already?'

Peggy looked at her. 'Perhaps not enough . . . not yet.'

They hugged. Peggy patted Jess's back. Jess smelt the faint, musty odour of Peggy's perspiration. It was really good to have someone to hold on to.

'Hey . . . ' Peggy held her at arm's length. She took a grubby piece of torn-up shirt from the pocket of her dungarees. She handed it to Jess to wipe her eyes. It smelt of donkey. 'How about that soup?'

Jess sniffed. Nodded. 'Why not?'

Jess slept in one of the downstairs rooms overlooking the valley. It was cavernous, cold, practically bare. A wide, shuttered bay window reached from the floor almost to the ceiling. Ice formed a hard shell along the bottom edges of the panes. Logs crackled and flared in the white marble fireplace.

On the high ceiling, grey cobwebs garlanded the moulded leaf cornices long made ugly and blurred by successive coatings of yellowed distemper.

The bed, a peeling veneered dressing table, Jess's suitcase, cassette player, a basket of logs . . . they were the only things in the room.

'You can sleep upstairs with me, if you like,' Peggy had said. 'It'll be warmer, two in a bed.'

Jess had been free to choose whichever room she liked best. 'No—I like the downstairs room.'

The house was on a hill. It had been built by a wealthy timber merchant at the turn of the century. It used to be painted white, the plaster now decayed and crumbling, blackened and peeling in places. When the sun went down, the elegant, west-facing bay windows were turned to blood.

'I bought it because I thought I could keep the animals downstairs and live upstairs. You know, like they did in medieval times,' Peggy had explained to Jess when she had visited there as a child.

Jess thought it sounded a great idea.

'But the bloody council wouldn't let me. Some crap about environmental health. Ridiculous . . . I keep my animals cleaner than some folk keep their houses. So I had the stables and pens put up. Cost me a damned fortune . . . '

Jess sat huddled in a blanket at the foot of the bed. Like one of those native Americans . . . the ones who believed they were descended from wolves. Her nose felt cold, like a knob of frost. Even her breathing echoed.

A pool of moonlight lay on the bare floor. A mist shrouded the forest treetops like disembodied lumps in an ocean of white.

In spite of the warmth of the blanket, Jess shivered. Coldness crept inside her bones.

Someone was watching . . . someone outside . . .

Jess rose and walked over to the window. Something seemed to be pulling her towards it. Something she couldn't resist. It was bitterly cold away from the fire. Her breath came out in a grey garland of silk. She touched the pane, drew a shape where it had misted the glass. She hugged the blanket tighter and shivered again. He was here, she was sure. The boy from the forest. The Gollum boy . . . Somewhere here in the tide of pale moonlight that swept the garden.

Outside, one of the dogs began to bark. Others followed. A whole cacophony of noise filled the night air. It went on for a minute or two then gradually died away. An answering bark, a haunting howl, came from the other side of the valley. There was a short high yelp from a young Labrador in one of the kennels. Then a kind of unearthly silence settled over the night.

Suddenly, from the barn, came the panic bleating of sheep.

Jess heard footsteps running down the uncarpeted staircase.

Her door flew open. Peggy stood on the threshold. The angel of death in a man's dark dressing-gown thrown over striped winceyette pyjamas and thick cardigan. Hair awry, standing on end as if she had been electrocuted. She held a shotgun.

'Quick, Jess. Something's at the Jacobs!'

The Jacobs! Peggy's pride and joy. There were a couple of other, ordinary sheep about the place. An old Romney ewe with a deformed leg, rescued from the slaughter house . . . a Sussex ram long past his usefulness. They lived companionably in the small home field behind the house but Peggy's beloved prize Jacobs were kept in the barn in cold weather. Her one indulgence amongst the motley assortment of abandoned and unwanted creatures.

Prize cattle slaughtered in frenzied attack . . .

Jess leapt up, dragged her coat from the bed. Peggy was already gone in a swirl of black wool. The air seemed to eddy in her wake.

Outside, the dogs had started kicking up again. Peggy was creeping round the side of the barn, weapon held in front like an old western gunslinger. She motioned to Jess.

'Push the door,' she hissed. 'The light switch's on the left.'

Through a crack Jess could see . . . hear . . . the Jacobs milling about. She jumped forward and threw open the barn door, clicked on the light.

Peggy darted forward to stand on the threshold, gun raised, legs apart.

A spear of moonlight fell across the floor. Above, Jess's eye caught a movement . . . a shifting of shadows . . . a hovering of reality. A blade of straw fluttered from the loft, through the moon-shaft, soft as a snowflake.

The sheep were quiet now, huddled in one corner, wide eyed. They began to disperse, heads down, munching.

Peggy relaxed. She lowered the shotgun. 'God, I thought it had got to be that damned creature. The forest beast they've been calling it.'

'The one that's been killing livestock?'

'Yes, how did you know?'

Jess told her about the newspaper. 'What do you think it is . . . a dog . . . dogs?'

Peggy shook her head.

'No . . . something a lot bigger, I reckon. I'd hate to shoot it but I'm afraid it could be the only way. You'd need experts to be here to tranquillize it if you wanted to capture it alive.'

'What do you think it is then?'

'I don't know.'

Peggy stomped around the barn. She glanced up into the hayloft. Jess held her breath.

'Could be a panther escaped from a zoo or a private collection. Could be a mountain lion, maybe,' Peggy went on. 'You'd be surprised how many people keep big cats.'

'In the paper it said . . . ' Jess blurted. 'There was a picture of a cow . . . mauled . . . I couldn't bear it.'

21

'Well, you know what the newspapers are, making a big deal of everything.'

'But it *is* a mystery.'

'Yes . . . come on, let's get back indoors before we freeze to death.'

'How do you think it got in?'

'I don't know, I'll check the timber in the morning. It may not even have been inside. Sheep can sense these things a mile off . . . and the dogs, I wondered what had set them off.'

'I could stay out here if you like? Keep watch,' Jess suggested. 'I'm not very sleepy.'

'Are you ever?'

Jess managed a grin. 'Sometimes.'

'You can if you want, although I don't think it'll come back now.'

'I'll stay a little while, just in case.'

Peggy frowned at her. 'You sure?'

Jess nodded. 'Yes.'

'Do you know how to use this?' Peggy held the gun towards her.

Jess grinned again.

'Oh yeah, everyone in respectable old Fairview Garden's got a shotgun.'

'Ha ha!'

Peggy showed her. 'If you do have to use it . . . remember it kicks back quite strongly . . . and make sure you keep the safety catch on.' She hesitated. 'Jess . . . ?'

'Don't worry, I'll be careful.'

Peggy looked relieved. 'Good. We don't want any more accidents.'

Jess fetched a horse blanket from the stable. She watched Peggy go in, saw the back door close . . . the light go on upstairs . . . then off again.

Jess stood by the barn doors, the blanket round her shoulders. The brittle moon hung in a blizzard of stars. It looked so close you could almost touch it. She sniffed the night air then turned, closed the doors and pulled the bar down inside.

She sat down on a bale of straw opposite the loft ladder. She looked up, eyes narrowed. He was there . . . somewhere . . . hiding amongst the straw bales.

'You can come down now,' she said, whispering. 'She's gone.'

2

LUC

Luc hesitated. He was still breathing heavily from his swift climb up to the hayloft. He peered out from between the bales. She was sitting opposite, staring upwards. She couldn't see him but she knew he was there.

Slowly he emerged. He brushed straw from his hair. He stood, looking down. She stared at him, eyes narrowed. He could see she was apprehensive.

Luc eyed the gun but it lay, untouched, beside her. She made no move towards it. He clambered down, jumping the last few metres. He landed on all fours and crouched, gazing sideways at her. Her green eyes stared at him, unwavering. He felt confused. Why hadn't she given him away? Why hadn't she let on to the woman he was in the hayloft? Her sharp, upward glance had told him she knew he was there the minute she came in. Had she sensed his fear? Did she know he had come only to see her?

He saw her swallow. She seemed determined not to let him know she was afraid. He almost smiled. Did she think she could hide it from him? Did she think she could hide anything? There was something in her eyes . . . he had seen it before when she had come to him in the forest. It was sorrow, loneliness . . . he recognized them both. They were like old, old ghosts that had haunted him for as long as he could remember.

Still holding her gaze, he raised his hand to his mouth, sucked where he had caught it on a splinter, climbing up. He tasted the warm, metallic taste of his blood.

Luc sat back on his haunches. The girl swallowed again then smiled uncertainly. She chewed her lip. He noticed how it reddened, the blood rising to the surface. She had a mouth slightly too big for her face. She pushed back one curl that had strayed across her eye. The colour of her hair reminded him of conkers, rubbed shiny, just ripe. That's how he had thought of her after that first time he'd seen her. The chestnut girl.

'What are you *doing* here?' she hissed.

How could he answer? That ever since he had seen her in the forest he had thought of nothing else? That his need to see her again was so great it was like a pain in his heart? She would think he was mad.

Luc had visited the place earlier. He had watched her through the kitchen window. He had seen the firelight dancing on her face. Once he thought she had spied him and he darted away. She had been upset about something and the woman had tried to comfort her. He sensed her despair. He had prowled around the house, explored. He had been here before, during daylight hours. He had come to see the wolf after he heard people talking about it in the shop. He had swallowed his fear. The woman who owned the place had been kind to him and he had learned, strangely, that there was nothing to be afraid of after all. But he had never returned . . . not until now.

There were many smells around the place. Dogs, horses, sheep, humans . . . a rat at the back of the store where they kept the animal feed. Other smells that left him puzzled. He had shivered in the darkness, in the keen wind of his curiosity.

'I . . . ' His voice came out in a high bark. He cleared his throat nervously and tried again. 'I just came in here to get warm . . . ' He wondered if she'd know he was lying. 'I am sorry I scared the sheep. I would not hurt them.'

'But what are you doing snooping round the house at this time of night?'

Again her eyes were pinning him down, forcing an explanation out of him where most people, puzzled and wary, left him to his own devices.

'I . . . I wanted to see you again.'

25

He got to his feet and sat on a straw bale, eyeing her cautiously. At his movement, he noticed the sheep bleated in fear, huddling in a corner. They were like the village people, huddling away, glancing over their shoulders, staring at him . . . whispering . . .

The girl rested her hands either side of her body and leaned forward. Her coat fell open and he could see her breasts straining at the thick cotton of her shirt. His mouth went dry. He ran his tongue, red, around his lips to moisten them. In spite of her rounded breasts she was thin. Too thin, as if the north wind might spirit her away.

A wave of her confusion reached out and touched him.

'Why didn't you just knock at the door like anyone else?' she asked.

He looked down, away from her green-eyed glance. The colour reminded him of spring buds, of the sharp-edged swords of bluebell leaves emerging. Her eyes were wide, and bright like a forest deer. He shrugged his shoulders. 'You would not have been very pleased . . . a stranger knocking at the door after dark.'

'You could have got shot. Peggy's fanatical about her Jacobs.'

'Yes.' He swallowed nervously. 'I'm sorry.' He rose to his feet and went to sit beside her. He could smell her, the scent of something sweet, something like herbs and spring flowers, drifted past his nostrils. He sniffed. It was something she washed her hair in. It reminded him of herbs that grew wild in the forest. He had seen her earlier through her bedroom window, brushing it in front of the mirror. He wanted to touch it, to know what it felt like.

'Forgive me?' he whispered.

She frowned. He felt her withdraw into herself. He was seeing his own face through her eyes. A pale, long-haired youth with gold-flecked eyes who looked as if he could be scared of his own sun-shadow. He seemed to feel her blood coursing through her veins. He frowned slightly . . . there was something wrong with her. An unmistakable sadness in

26

her eyes. There was something else too. Hate? Not for him but for someone else. Who . . . or what . . . he did not know. He could only see she was caught in some kind of trap, held fast, and that her need to be free was as great as his own.

'Forgive you,' she giggled. 'That's a weird thing to say.'

'Is it?'

'You just scared us, that's all. We thought—'

Her fingers sought and found and unconsciously twisted the silver chain at her neck. Attached to the chain was a locket in the shape of a heart.

Luc cleared his throat hastily. 'What . . . what did you think?'

'We thought it might be that animal that's killing livestock. Did you see the story in the paper?'

He nodded. His heart thudded unevenly. She had seen it too . . . everyone must have seen it. 'Yes.' He swallowed again. 'Does anyone know what kind of animal it is?'

'No, I don't think so. My aunt thinks it might be a puma or something. You know, something escaped from a zoo.'

'What makes her think that?'

The girl winced. 'The way it tears its prey to pieces, I suppose.'

He smiled at the absurdity of it. The girl stiffened, looked angry. 'Well, it could be. That photo in the paper was terrible.' She looked stricken, as if it was someone, some*thing*, she loved that the creature had killed.

He realized suddenly . . . that's what it was. Something . . . someone she loved *had* died.

'Is that it?' he asked softly.

She looked confused. 'Is what . . . what?'

'You have lost someone you love . . . yes?'

He heard her gasp. Her hand flew to her throat.

'How on earth . . . ?'

'I am sorry,' he said. 'I can see it in your eyes.'

She lowered her gaze. 'I didn't know it showed that much.'

'Yes,' he said. 'It does.'

27

He looked down. His hands were twisting themselves together in his lap. His jeans were muddy, dusty where he had been lying in the straw. He picked an ear of corn wedged behind a stud on the sleeve of his leather jacket. He flicked his hair back from his face and swallowed noisily.

He looked at her again. Her face had gone pale, her pupils swam in a wash of tears.

Luc tried to explain. 'I could tell by your eyes that you have felt deep sadness. And what is more sad than when someone you love dies?'

She was suddenly on the defensive, not believing him.

'I bet you heard me talking to Peggy.'

'No, I could just sense it. Truly, it is not difficult to see.'

She made to stand up. 'You're weird,' she said angrily. 'You'd better go.'

He didn't answer.

'Doesn't anyone . . . your mother . . . worry if you're out in the forest at night, for goodness' sake?'

He felt laughter bubble up. 'My mother?' he exclaimed, incredulous that the girl should even know of her existence. 'My mother . . . worry about me out at night? You are joking, no?'

The girl flushed. 'No, I'm serious.' She sat down again.

His hand shook slightly as he put out a finger tentatively to touch a tendril of her hair. She jerked her head away. He drew his hand back quickly.

'What do you know about my mother?' he asked softly, pretending he had not noticed her withdrawal.

The girl shrugged and pushed her hair back with bird hands. 'Nothing—just that you live with her in Gol—'

He raised one eyebrow, smiled. 'Where?'

'Um. Peggy calls your house Gollum Castle,' she confessed. He could see roses of embarrassment on her cheeks. ' . . . sorry.' She looked down at her lap.

'Gollum? The ring-stealer?'

'Yes.' She stared back at him, looking surprised that he knew.

'Why does she call it that?'

The girl explained.

Luc grinned, then laughed. 'It is a very good description.'

The girl relaxed. She smiled into his eyes. Luc saw her mouth wasn't too big at all. He let his gaze linger on her lips.

'You have been talking about me then?' It was more of a statement than a question. He looked at her eyes again.

She hung her head. 'Peggy said . . . What's your name?' she asked suddenly. She had a way of looking at him that made him feel as if he was the only other living person in the world.

'Luc,' he said. 'With a "c". It is French. My ancestors were . . . French.'

'Yes. Peggy told me.'

He raised his eyebrows. What else had the woman told her, he wondered?

'Mine's Jess,' she said.

'Jess,' he repeated softly. His heart skipped a wild beat. 'Jessica . . . it means the wealthy one.'

'Does it?' She laughed. 'How did you know that?'

'I read it in a book. I know you are sad too.' He reached out a finger to touch her again.

She lowered her eyes but didn't pull away. 'Yes,' she mumbled. 'You've already told me.'

'What else has the woman . . . Peggy, told you about me?'

'Nothing much. Just that you live with your mother . . . that she never goes out . . . you have to do the shopping . . . things like that.'

Luc snorted air through his nostrils. 'That just shows you what lies people tell,' he said. He curled his lip. 'Those village people . . . they hate me . . . '

'No . . . ' she said quickly. 'I'm sure they don't hate you. They're just wary of anyone who . . . who's different.'

'Why do they tell the lies then?' he asked bitterly.

'Lies . . . what lies?'

He shrugged. 'Very well, then . . . stories . . . It is not true what they say about my mother.'

'I'm sorry,' the girl said. 'I'm just telling you what Peggy told me.'

'Perhaps . . . ' Luc hesitated. 'Perhaps . . . one day . . . I will take you to meet her.'

'OK,' she said.

He smiled. 'But for now . . . please . . . would you come for a walk with me?'

'You're nuts.' She moved further away from him now. Suddenly, as if reminded of the fact there might be something to be cautious about.

'Nuts?' he repeated, frowning, not understanding what she meant.

'Yes . . . crazy if you think I'm going for a walk with some guy I've never met before. I'm not that barmy.'

'We have met before,' he said. 'You know we have.' He swallowed again. He was gaining courage. He could see she was not like the others. She was wary of him, yes . . . but not afraid. He saw her confusion again and laughed inwardly because she knew he was right. That their meeting had been fate. He knew for certain now. She would be the one.

'You scarpered,' she said. 'When I saw you in the forest.'

'Scarpered . . . ' he repeated. 'Sorry . . . I . . . ?'

'You ran away,' she explained with a smile. 'You scarpered.'

He lowered his eyes. He pulled at the hairs on the back of his hand. He raised his eyes again to her face.

'Why?' she asked. 'Why did you run away? I . . . I wanted to talk to you.'

'You startled me,' he lied. He didn't want her to know he had not had the courage to face her then. She would really think he was . . . what did she say . . . nuts? 'Fight or flight . . . you know . . . '

'Do you study psychology as well as the meaning of names?' she asked.

'I study many things,' he said.

'Well, as a matter of fact you scared me too!' she said hotly. Coals burned in her eyes. 'I didn't know there would be anyone else about.'

'Yes, you did. You knew I was there.'

Confusion marred her face. She looked down. Her lashes were like butterflies hovering on her cheeks. 'I thought you were just . . . shy,' she said.

'Shy?' He frowned. 'Oh, yes. I am very shy.'

She stared at him. Then she said, 'Look, you really had better go. Peggy—'

'What would she do? Chase me away. Set the dogs on me? Don't worry, I am used to it.'

'Why?'

'Why what?'

'Why do people chase you away?'

'They do not like me . . . I told you.'

'No one knows you, do they?'

'No,' he replied. 'No one knows me at all.'

She stared at him but said nothing.

'How about that walk?' He got down on his knees and took her hand in his own. This time she didn't pull away. 'Please.' He tilted his head to one side.

She pulled her hand from his. 'Get up, twit,' she said, smiling. He could see he had won her. 'You're nutty as a fruit cake. Look, you really had better go.'

'You will not walk with me, then?' He could not bear to let her go . . . not yet.

'Luc . . . it's the middle of the night for God's sake.'

'Are you frightened of the dark?'

She shook her head. 'No, but that doesn't mean I want to go swanning off into the forest in the middle of the night, does it?'

'The forest is wonderful at night,' he said, looking at her through his mane of wild hair. He got to his feet and sat down beside her again. He tucked his hair back behind his ears. 'It is beautiful . . . especially this winter time of year—' He broke off. He was thinking of another time he had been

31

in the forest at night. It had been one of those misty, autumn evenings . . . that dusk-time . . . half day . . . half night when you weren't sure if shadows were real, if moving patterns of shade were illusions or reality. He had pursued the trail all the way through the valley, across the clearing then down along the forest ride. But by the river bank he had lost it, the search was fruitless. He had been too late. He was always just too late . . .

Luc came back to reality. Jess was still staring at him. 'Well . . . ' he said quickly. 'Will you come with me? There is no need to be afraid.' He was trying to be gentle. He thought it would be a mistake to show how anxious he was . . . how desperate.

'Luc . . . I can't,' she murmured as if she was under his spell. He saw she could not take her eyes from his face.

He held out his hand. 'Come on, Jess.'

She shook her head. Temptation was like an aura round her hair. His nostrils flared. She had thought her life was worth nothing but she was wrong. It was worth everything . . . to him.

'Look, I'm sorry, I really can't.' Her face lit up suddenly. 'Hey, why don't you come tomorrow. Peggy won't mind, she said you'd been here before.'

'Yes, I came to see Sleet.' Luc felt a pang of sadness. He had loved the wild creature . . . wanted him desperately. The wolf had been lonely too, padding up and down in that cage when he should have been free. 'She sent him away.'

'He needed to be with other wolves.'

'I know, but he would not have been lonely with me. Wolves are not the evil killers they are made out to be, you know? All that is a myth. They are beautiful creatures. I asked the woman if I could have him but she would not let me.'

'She didn't tell me that.'

'Did she not?'

'She probably forgot. She's a bit . . . scatty.'

32

'Yes.'

'She showed me a picture of him.'

'I would like to see it . . . Jess.' He lingered over her name. It sounded beautiful to him, like the whisper of wind through trees.

'I'm sure Peggy wouldn't mind . . . '

'Tomorrow?'

'If you like.'

'Very well.'

'Honestly,' Jess stood up, 'I can't just go for a walk with you, not just like that, not in the middle of the night.'

He nodded. 'I understand.'

He had been hoping for too much. His dreams had intruded on reality, as usual.

'How did you really know?' she asked, closing the barn door. He helped her put the bar across.

'Know what?'

'About . . . about Danny?'

So that had been his name. The one who had died. Luc curled his lip in the darkness. He was glad Danny had died. He had the feeling she would not be here otherwise.

'I told you, it shows in your eyes.'

'I honestly didn't realize it was that obvious.'

Luc shrugged. 'Maybe not to everyone . . . but to me, it is.'

'Your house,' Jess said, 'where exactly is it?'

Luc pointed down the slope towards the forest edge. 'Just the other side,' he said. 'You can get to it from the main road but I prefer the forest paths.'

'Has it got a proper name?'

'Yes,' he said, 'Spital House.'

Jess frowned. 'That's a weird name.'

'There has been a dwelling there,' he shrugged, 'for hundreds of years. The name means refuge from wolves. The Anglo-Saxons put them up for travellers. My own family have lived there for . . . ' he shrugged, 'more than two hundred years.'

'Were there wolves here in the forest, then?' she interrupted. He could see she was fascinated. The way she looked at him made his spine shiver.

'When my family came here?' he shrugged. 'No, I do not think so. But there were wolves in Scotland up until the eighteenth century . . . in France, until the middle of the nineteenth.' He touched her gently under the chin. 'I will tell you about them one day if you like.'

She did not answer but he knew she could not resist.

He felt her eyes following as he ran off down the hill. The grass beneath his feet crunched with frost. The air was sharp, brittle with moonshine. A rabbit ran across his path, criss-crossing in panic. Its tail bobbed, a snowdrop in the light. Somewhere in the forest, a vixen called. Her harsh cry echoing eerily through the stillness of the night.

Luc suddenly realized he had not eaten all day. He had been preoccupied . . . busy with thoughts of the girl he had seen in the forest. He swallowed the saliva that threatened to spill from his mouth and clenched his aching jaws together. He ran home as fast as he could, plunging through the undergrowth, lashing at the overhanging twigs that set snares against his flight.

At home, the place was in darkness, empty. The tower reared black against the sky. He thought he saw a shadow move across his vision. A swirling, amorphous mass of grey mist. As he watched, it seemed to gather together . . . to form into a shape. Luc covered his eyes. He groaned in agony. When he looked again the mist had gone.

Luc crept into the empty house. He found the remains of a stew in the pantry and sat to eat it by the cold and empty fireplace. The darkness folded itself around him . . . made him feel safe. Even that sensation sent shivers of fear across his heart. Was he getting like her? Relishing the darkness like a saviour? Then he thought of Jess. It was going to be all right. She was definitely the one. She *cared* about him . . .

he could read it in her eyes. He wondered if she would still care about him when she knew the truth. Or if she would ever believe him?

Luc picked the newspaper up off the floor. There it was, the glaring headline, *Prize cattle slaughtered in frenzied attack*. He wondered if his mother had been down here reading it. He lit the lamp then went to the drawer and took out a pair of scissors. He carefully cut out the story. Then he took a large book from the cupboard in the chimney breast and placed the cutting inside. He did not stop to read the others that were already in there. He knew them almost by heart. Besides, they frightened him . . . scared him half to death.

Luc pushed his hands through his hair. 'Jess . . . Jess . . .' He said her name aloud. 'You must help me . . . '

Luc covered his face with his hands. He felt tears well up and spill. He wiped them away angrily. He had decided he was a child no longer . . . tears were for children.

He stood up, angry with himself. He caught sight of his reflection, lamplit and misty in the grimy mirror over the fireplace. He peered closer, at the amber-coloured eyes, the long mane of wild hair. He ran his fingers over his jaw. His skin was rough with the day's growth of beard. He glanced down at the long, golden hairs that grew on the back of his hand. He looked again at his reflection. The image seemed to change before his eyes . . . become distorted . . . the skin blemished . . . the eyebrows thick and dark. He gave a sudden, wild cry. In a mad gesture of despair he picked up the poker that lay on the hearth and smashed it into the mirror. Fragments flew like silver rain. One caught his cheek. He felt the sharp sting of pain, the blood well to the surface. He crouched to the floor, his arms over his head and burst into a wild and uncontrollable frenzy of tears.

3

JESS

Jess was in the kitchen, huddled by the stove, waiting for the kettle to boil. For the first time in months, Danny hadn't been the first person she thought about when she awoke.

Peggy was emptying the ashcan. A blast of cold air blew in as she opened the back door.

Jess absently took hold of the grubby teacloth. She began drying the mound of dishes that had been stacked on the draining board since the day before yesterday. She felt groggy, still tired. She had wandered all night in a limbo land between sleeping and waking.

Once she had heard a voice. It was her own. They say it's the first sign, talking to yourself. What was it she'd said? A name? Danny? Luc? She frowned, trying to remember.

Luc . . . ?

She remembered the way he looked at her. The way he had seen her soul. What kind of person came to ask you to go for a walk in the middle of a cold January night, for God's sake?

January . . . the wolf month. Wolf-monath . . .

Jess frowned and bit her lip. She'd read that somewhere . . . that book on myths and legends Peggy sent her for her fifteenth birthday.

Beneath his buckskin leather jacket, Luc had worn the thin, grey sweatshirt and jeans he'd worn in the forest. The sweatshirt was faded and torn. It looked as if it came from the Oxfam shop. Beneath his clothes, she sensed lean, vigorous muscles. His jeans, tight across his hips and thighs, were torn and muddy at the knees as if he had scrambled through undergrowth on all fours. His fingers had been strong, warm, when hers had felt almost frozen. His long, wild hair was goldlit in the overhead light of the barn. His smile was slightly crooked, eye-teeth longer than normal. There was something elemental about him, as if he belonged to the wild. He reminded her of a forest creature, muscles tensed for flight. He seemed rigid with suppressed motion, the string of a bow drawn tight.

Even now, thinking about him, Jess shivered. *Eyes of autumn forests and shadows.*

Where did eyes that colour come from? And what was it she saw in them? A mixture of fear, of longing . . . Yet when she stared, full into his face, his gaze had fallen away, shyly, as if her eyes had burned him. It was crazy but he knew about Danny. He *knew* about Danny. Did it really show that much? Unless he really did have some inner instinct to sense people's feelings. Like a dog, Peggy would say. She said dogs were more sensitive to moods than human beings. Unless Luc was some kind of medium—a person who knew what you were like, just from the aura that surrounded you. Maybe that's what he was? Some kind of spirit guide . . . a young man from nowhere . . . ?

'It's going to snow.' Peggy came back indoors, slamming the door shut against the wind.

'That'll be fun.' Jess came to. She stacked the dishes away.

'Glad you think so.' Peggy shoved the ashcan back into the stove. 'It looks pretty but it just makes life here tougher for everybody.'

'I'm here to help.'

Peggy smiled. 'Yes, of course you are, darling girl. I can see I'll get spoilt, having you around. You know the animals really like you.'

'I love them too. I always remember that Alsatian you had when I came to stay with you before. I really wanted to take him home. Do you remember?'

Peggy grinned. 'Your mum said he would make too much mess.'

Jess turned down the corners of her mouth. 'She thinks everyone makes too much mess.'

Peggy laughed.

'I love animals because they don't try to tell you what to do,' said Jess. 'And they accept you for what you are. People are always trying to change each other, make you into something different.'

'Very shrewd observation for one so young,' Peggy said with a wry grin. She gave Jess a hug. 'I really love having you here, Jess.'

'Mum said a few weeks here and I'd be dying to get back.'

'To the home comforts . . . central heating?'

Jess shrugged. 'Who knows what she meant?'

'How long did you stay in the barn last night?'

'Not long, it was freezing.' Jess wasn't going to tell her about Luc. Even Peggy, with her ideas on personal freedom, wouldn't relish the thought of a peeping Tom.

'The sheep were OK?'

'Yes.'

'I meant to tell you,' Peggy said. 'I keep a small revolver upstairs in case of intruders. Don't worry, I've got a licence. I have to keep the shotgun locked in its cabinet in the hall but I like to have something on hand. You can't be too careful.'

'No,' Jess agreed. The papers were full of people breaking in, raping . . . killing women alone in the house.

'It's under my bed. I thought you ought to know, just in case.'

She must have seen Jess's expression.

'Don't get paranoid though, will you? I'm sure we're safe as houses. It's just a precaution. Remind me, I'll show you how to use it.'

'OK,' Jess said.

Outside, a pale sun was beginning to emerge. Jess stared out of the window at grey and orange clouds. The skeleton trees were black against the brightening sky.

Peggy put on her duffle coat, pushed her feet into muddy wellingtons. A cockerel crowed from the henhouse.

'I'd better get on. Help yourself to breakfast.'

'Thanks, I'm starving.' Jess had almost forgotten what it was like.

'Really?' Peggy said, eyebrows raised.

'Yes, really,' Jess laughed. 'I must be getting better.'

'Yes. Well have as much as you like.'

'Thanks.'

Jess made porridge. She poured on rich, creamy milk, a dark sprinkling of brown sugar. It tasted great but she couldn't finish it all. Too much and she'd throw up.

She ran outside to scrape the remains on to the bird table. Underneath was a dead sparrow. Jess bent to pick up the pathetic bundle of feathers. Its head was almost severed, black blood dried like dark toffee.

'Bloody cats,' Jess said angrily. She took the corpse into the kitchen. She threw it into the stove, watching with morbid fascination as a holocaust of flames devoured the tiny body.

The phone rang.

It was Emma.

'God, what a time to ring,' Jess said.

'I'm going out this evening. How's things?'

'Fine,' Jess said automatically.

'What have you been doing with yourself?'

'Nothing much, looking after the animals, stacking logs, trying to keep warm, you know?' Jess was surprised when what sounded like a laugh came from her throat.

'It doesn't exactly sound a bundle of fun.'

'It's great. No parents giving you worried looks. No one to order you around. Actually I have met someone you might find interesting.'

'Wow, who?'

'A guy. His name's Luc.'

39

'I thought your aunt lived in the middle of nowhere?'

'She does. I think he comes from nowhere.'

Jess went on to explain.

'He sounds a bit of a weirdo.'

'Yes, he is a bit, although I think he's just shy and lonely. There's just him and his mother. He's never even been to school.'

Jess heard Emma laugh. 'Lucky thing. Do you fancy him then?'

Jess's heart twisted in a knot of betrayal. 'Come off it, Emma. You know I still . . . love . . . Danny.'

'Oh, Jess, you can't love a dead person . . . not for ever.'

'Six months isn't for ever.'

'Jess, it's too long. You know, Danny—'

'Shut up, Emma. Did you phone to give me a lecture? I came here to get away from all that.'

'I know, I'm sorry. I miss you, Jess.'

'Me too,' Jess said.

'Everyone sends their love.'

'Have you seen . . . ?' Jess could hardly say the name. 'Charlene?'

'Um . . . yes . . . yesterday.'

'Where?'

'She's back working in the shop.'

'Did she say anything?'

'No.' Jess could imagine Emma shaking her head, her cropped, spiky hair stiff with hair gel. 'I don't think she recognized me. I only popped in for a mag., she was busy with another customer anyway.'

'I just wondered . . . '

'Jess, you've got to stop thinking about it.'

'I know.'

'She's not likely to say anything to me, anyway, is she?'

Jess shrugged. 'No, I suppose not.'

'Look, Jess, I've got to go,' Emma said. 'Mum's yelling from downstairs. She's giving me a lift.'

'Don't forget I want copies of your notes.'

'I won't. Call me, Jess, tell me how you're getting on with Monsieur Luc.' She attempted a French accent.

'He's supposed to be coming here later, we're going for a walk.'

'Doesn't sound very exciting.'

'No,' Jess said.

Jess stood by the phone, biting her lip. She breathed hard. It still hurt. Knowing about Danny and that girl, Charlene. So she was back working in the paper shop? Jess had thought it was all lies at first. That was until she saw her at the funeral. Hate still hovered on the edge of Jess's mind. Still killing her, eating her up . . . She wondered if Luc had seen that too?

The telephone shrilled again. Jess almost leapt from her skin. Her hand hovered over the receiver, then fell back to her side. Her mother had the habit of ringing early. Today, like all the others, there was nothing to say.

On the mantelpiece was the Polaroid of the wolf, Sleet. Jess took it down. She stared at it for a moment then put it into the back pocket of her jeans.

She bundled herself into scarf and coat, pulled one of Peggy's woolly hats down almost to her eyebrows and went outside.

Frost lay like icing on the grass. The whole valley was sheathed in silver. Jess drew a deep breath. The sharp air cut her lungs like a blade.

'I've turned the ponies out,' Peggy called. 'Take that bale of hay down to them, would you, Jess? Old Barney the ram and the ewe need some as well. I'm just going to check the Jacobs.'

'OK.'

There were footprints, scuffing the frozen grass. They led down the slope towards the forest. Jess could see them, like tramlines weaving.

Luc . . .

41

He was still there in her mind. His long-legged gait as he left her. His animal grace. Long hair rippling as he ran. His moon-shadowed figure disappearing towards the night forest. How on earth he found the paths she did not know. He carried no torch, nothing. Jess had the feeling those topaz eyes could probably see in the dark.

Going indoors she had heard a curious noise. A cry. Almost, but not quite, human. It had sent spiders scuttling down her spine.

Jess opened the field gate and pushed the barrow through. The three ponies galloped up the slope towards her, manes tossing. By the water trough lay a dead rabbit. Its neck was twisted, broken, although there was no other sign of injury.

With a small cry, Jess picked it up. Its coat was frozen stiff, fur matted in spikes. The head lolled, dislocated. The eyes were still open, shot with blood. Jess touched its nose tenderly. Her eyes pricked with tears.

Everything around was death.

Everything . . .

'What's that?' Peggy called from the barn doorway, breaking the spell.

Jess laid the rabbit down on the hard, rutted ground.

'A rabbit,' she called. She wiped the back of her glove across her nose and lugged the bale off the barrow. She cut the string, scattering hay for the impatient horses. The grey took a mouthful, pulling it from the bale and tossing it up like a gored bullfighter. He laid back his ears and kicked out at the animal behind.

'Hey.' Jess slapped him on the flank. 'Don't be a pig. Skedaddle, you!' She pushed him away. The smaller ponies barged through.

'Is it mangled?' Peggy called.

'No.'

'Bring it. I'll cook it for the dogs. No sense in wasting it.'

'That's strange,' Peggy said later, examining the corpse.

'Its neck's broken but there's no other sign of injury. I wonder what happened?'

'I heard a really weird cry last night just as I was coming back indoors. Do rabbits make a noise?'

'If they're caught in a trap, yes. A noise like bloody hell. But this hasn't been in a trap. Maybe you heard a vixen. They sound really spooky at night.'

Jess frowned. 'Maybe.'

'Where did you find the rabbit?'

'It was by the trough, perhaps it ran into it?'

Peggy shrugged. 'Running in panic from something, I reckon. Probably that fox you heard.'

'Probably,' Jess said. 'I'll start mucking out if you like.'

'Great,' Peggy said. 'I'll give you a hand in a minute.'

The radio was on in the stable, the local station blaring out pop. They cut off The Rolling Stones for a newsflash.

'Hear that?' Peggy stood by the door.

'What?' Jess had been miles away. Reliving one of those precious moments with Danny that seemed, strangely, to have suddenly become elusive. Like a vivid dream that fades with time.

'That animal's killed again. That's the fourth time this winter.'

'Oh, no! What this time?'

'Listen.' Peggy turned up the volume.

'The attack on Mrs Mason's goat was vicious and frenzied,' the newsreader said. 'The animal was dragged from its shelter and literally torn to pieces. The police have no idea how its killer managed to get in. Mrs Mason said the door was fastened securely . . . '

Jess put her fingers over her ears. 'Switch it off, Peggy, I can't bear it.'

The pictures came in flashes, like an old black and white silent movie. The carcass of the dead cow . . . film Jess had seen of drowned and bloated oxen after floods in Bangladesh . . . a story of a fox cub torn to bloody shreds by terriers . . . Danny's twisted body, the pool of blood

43

seeping . . . the sparrow . . . the rabbit . . . *In the midst of life we are in death.*

'Hang on . . . ' Peggy was saying.

'Police are asking local farmers and pet owners to be vigilant and to phone their local police station if they have any information that might help throw some light on the mystery. The creature's behaviour seems to mirror that of the legendary Surrey puma and the Exmoor beast. There are various theories as to what kind of animal *this* one could be. All previous efforts to track the creature down have failed. It just seems to vanish into thin air. We spoke on the telephone earlier to veterinary surgeon, Jack Stride.'

Peggy listened for a minute or two longer then switched off the radio.

'I bet that's what upset the dogs last night,' she said, 'and the sheep. I knew something was up.' She pressed her lips together in a tight, worried line. 'What the hell can it be?'

'I don't know,' Jess said, scared.

'We'd better double check all the doors tonight.'

'It sounds as if it can unfasten doors.'

Peggy snorted. 'Don't let your imagination run away with you, sweetie. I expect that daft old bitch with the goats forgot to shut it up properly.'

As she spoke, a Land Rover pulled into the yard. A tall man in a waxed jacket and tweed flat cap got out.

'Where are you, Peg?' he shouted.

'Here, Jack. In the stable!'

Jess was sure this time. A flush did come to Peggy's cheeks as she heard the man call out.

'Jack . . . hi!' Peggy went out to meet him. She linked her arm through his and brought him into the stable. 'Jess, this is Jack Stride, the vet I was telling you about. We've just been hearing you on the radio, Jack.'

But you didn't say he was your lover, Jess almost said. Peggy's affection for the man shone as clear as day.

'Hi.' Jess shook the proffered hand. Jack's grip was warm

and strong. Deep-set brown eyes smiled into hers.

'I've heard all about you,' Jack said.

'Yeah?'

'Don't worry . . . it's all been good.'

Peggy smiled up at him. 'You're getting quite famous.'

Jack snorted.

'Jack was on the radio once before,' Peggy explained to Jess. 'He was talking about a mastiff that had run off from one of the boarding kennels on the other side of the village. The owner was desperate to get her back.'

'Did they find her?' Jess asked.

'Not until months later,' Jack said. 'She turned up at her own home. We think someone might have taken her off in a car. Dogs do that, you know. They sometimes travel miles to find their home. No one really knows how they do it.'

'Yes,' said Jess, 'I've heard about that.'

'They've broadcast the warning about the creature twice already this morning,' Jack said. 'People will be getting panicky.' He turned to Peggy. 'The local bobby's trying to get up a posse to hunt it down. The RSPCA chaps are anxious it shouldn't be harmed. I wondered if you'd fancy coming along?'

'When?'

'Next time it kills or if anyone spots it. They forecast snow for several days . . . it should be easy to track.'

Jess felt an unaccountable stab of fear. 'It would be terrible if you had to kill it,' she said.

'I'd like to think we could capture it alive. It depends.'

'On what?'

'On what kind of creature it is. How near we can get. You need to get quite close to shoot tranquillizers.'

Jess nodded. 'I see.'

'If it's a big cat, and I've got a sneaking feeling that's what it is, it'll be as crafty as hell.'

'You know there's been stories about this kind of thing all over the country,' Peggy said. 'And abroad. We might never catch up with it.'

'I know. But whatever these beasts are, they come close to human habitation in winter when food is scarce, then disappear up into the hills, or moors, during the summer. We've got to try and get it while it's hungry, otherwise we might never have another chance. It could roam for miles in summer and start its pattern of killing somewhere else next year.'

'By which time everyone will have forgotten about it,' Peggy said.

'Probably.' Jack grinned.

'I saw a programme on TV,' Jess said. 'About a black panther in the West Country. At least, that's what people thought it was.'

'Right. The Exmoor beast. They've never caught it,' Jack said grimly.

'Do you think that's what our creature could be?' It seemed funny to call it that . . . our creature . . . as if it belonged to them.

'Who knows,' Jack shrugged. 'But whatever it is, the sooner we find it, the better. No one can afford to lose livestock in this way.'

'Something disturbed the dogs last night,' Peggy said. 'And scared the Jacobs. We came out but didn't find anything.'

'Footprints?'

Peggy shook her head. 'Did you see any, Jess?'

They both turned to look at her. 'No,' Jess said, the lie falling guiltily from her lips. 'Nothing.'

Peggy took Jack's arm again. 'Come on in, I'll make some coffee. Jess?'

Jess shook her head. 'No, I'm fine. I'll do the dogs' food.'

Peggy gave her a hug. 'Isn't she great, Jack? God knows what I'll do without her when she goes back home.'

Maybe I won't go back. Maybe I'll stay here . . . for ever? Perhaps I'll end up like Luc's mother, a hermit?

* * *

46

She was in the feedstore, measuring out food for the dogs. She was thinking about Luc. How she had seen him in the forest. How he had been sitting there in the clearing, blending in with his background as if he was part of the landscape itself.

She heard whines, frantic barking from the kennels. Behind her she heard shuffled feet, the sound of someone breathing.

'Oh!' Jess said, turning. 'You made me jump.'

'I said I would come today.'

He was standing in the doorway, pallid cheeks flushed, smiling uncertainly. He wore a ragged combat jacket. His unruly hair was tied back. The long pony-tail drifting softly over one shoulder. Jess noticed stark cheekbones, a haunted look. There was the red scar of a cut on his cheek. She wondered how he'd got it. It hadn't been there when she saw him last night. He seemed different in the daylight. Somehow more human. Just like a rather scruffy, shy, beautiful boy in need of a friend. He looked uneasy in spite of his smile.

'I'm busy right now.' Her heart pounded. Why did she say that? Why was she so scared of the effect he was having on her?

'I'm sorry. You did not say what the best time would be...'

She lugged the bag of dried dog food off the counter and put it back in the feed bin. She filled a jug with water.

'Didn't I? I'm sorry, I should have said in the afternoon. We have a lot to do in the mornings.'

'What is that?' He indicated the dog meal.

'Food for the dogs.'

He came forward, poked his finger into the dried meal. 'It looks terrible. Do they not get meat?'

Jess made a face. 'It does, doesn't it. They seem to like it though. It's full of vitamins and stuff. Some've been starved, they're glad of anything.' She tipped a measured amount of water into each bowl. 'We mix meat with it when Peggy can afford to buy it.'

'Come for that walk with me?'

Jess fiddled with her glove, then looked at him, knowing she would give in. 'I'm really busy.' She felt the light touch of his finger on her arm.

'You said . . . '

She stared at him. 'OK. But I'd better tell Peggy.'

'You have to have her permission?' He bent to look at her face.

She smiled. 'Do you mind, I am an adult. She might have some more jobs for me, that's all.'

'I saw her go indoors with that man. They had their arms round each other.'

'Were you watching?'

'Yes. I waited till they had gone.'

'Why? They don't bite.'

He smiled again. 'No.'

'I think they're in love,' Jess confessed. 'She didn't tell . . . ' she broke off. Why was she saying this? What was it about him that made her want to pour her heart out?

'What did she not tell you?' He was looking at her again, his eyes boring holes in her skull.

'That she was sleeping with somebody.'

He frowned. 'Sleeping . . . ?'

'Yes, making love . . . you know.'

'It bothers you, yes?'

'No, why should it?'

He spread large hands. 'You tell me?'

She drew herself together. 'Oh, I don't know. I just didn't think she had anybody, that's all. Come on,' she said, suddenly impatient. 'Let's tell them we're off.'

He hovered on the doorstep. 'You go. I shall wait.'

'Don't be daft,' she dragged his arm.

'No, really, I would rather not.' She saw fear, wariness, in his eyes. What a strange kind of life he must live, to be afraid of meeting people this way? He was like his mother, she supposed.

She shrugged. 'OK, please yourself. Oh . . . ' she fumbled in her back pocket. 'Here.' She handed him the Polaroid.

When she came out he was still looking at it. There was a curious expression on his face. Jess thought it looked like love. It wasn't until later she realized he'd kept it.

'OK,' she said. 'Let's go.'

They went through the gate into the field. The ponies lifted their heads, eyes wide, white. They galloped off, manes, tails held high, streaming in the wind.

'They're nutty, those ponies,' Jess remarked. 'One minute they're tame as anything, the next they gallop off as if the hounds of the Baskervilles are after them.'

Luc said nothing. He was looking at her as they walked down the hill. She wondered what he was thinking.

Once, she slipped on the frozen grass. He caught her arm, steadied her, then let it go.

'Where are we going?' Jess wasn't at all sure she was doing the right thing. Going off with him. A stranger.

He took her hand. She felt his fingers encircling hers. Long nails digging in her palm. The back of his hand was scratched as if he'd been plunging through undergrowth.

She had a job keeping up with his long strides.

'Hey,' she laughed stupidly. 'Slow down, what's the rush?'

He looked repentant. 'Sorry, I am used to running most of the time.' He glanced over his shoulder as if suspicious someone might be following.

'Are you a keep-fit fanatic?'

'What?'

She repeated the question but he only shrugged. He didn't even seem to know what she meant.

She looked at him. 'How did you cut your cheek?'

His fingers flew to the scar. 'I broke a mirror.'

'That's seven years bad luck.'

'Who said?'

'It's an old superstition . . . have you never heard it?'

'No,' he said.

They walked through the frozen forest. Leaves crunched beneath their feet, fragile with frost. A pheasant darted in front, red neck feathers like a splash of blood. Jess felt Luc suddenly jerk forward as if he wanted to run after it. She was aware of his lean body beside her, his arm brushing her shoulder, their strides now in rhythm. Dark, naked branches clicked overhead, skeletal against the leaden sky. She felt his glance.

'Your hair,' he said suddenly. 'It reminds me of conkers.'

She laughed, not knowing whether to be flattered or insulted. 'Thanks very much!'

'Conkers are beautiful.' Jess felt his fingers move over hers. 'Rich . . . shiny . . . have you ever really looked at one?'

Jess admitted she hadn't.

'You should.' He raised his face to the wind and sniffed. 'It is going to snow. I can smell it.'

She sniffed too. 'Yes.' She smiled at him. 'So can I.'

The forest track divided in two. The left fork led off into dense woodland. Luc pulled her to the right. 'This way.' He was pulling her. 'It is slippery and dangerous near the caves. This way is best.'

She held back. 'Where are we going? I'm not sure if I . . . '

His face fell. 'I was going to show you Gollum Castle.'

Jess tilted her head sideways, frowning at him. Then she dropped her eyes. 'I think I should get back.'

'What are you scared of?'

She examined a hole in her glove. 'I'm not scared,' she fibbed.

Luc was looking at her, reading her. 'You could tell me about him if you like,' he said.

Her eyes flew wide. 'What?'

'On the way . . . you could tell me about the person who died. What was his name? Danny?'

Jess breathed heavily, angrily. 'There's nothing to tell.' She flushed at the lie. Why was she afraid to tell him? Sometimes it's better to talk to strangers. God knows, there hadn't really been anyone else. Peggy was kind but she was a different generation. There had been Emma, of course.

But Jess knew exactly what Emma had thought of Danny. Maybe if she told someone, really told them the whole story, it would stop her going crazy?

He was pulling her again. 'Come on,' he insisted. 'We will walk there then I will walk back with you. It will not hurt, will it?'

'No.'

The forest smelt of damp earth, decaying leaves. Branches clicked, squeaked in conversation with the winter wind. They were walking up a gentle incline. The rise in the ground led to the clearing. Frost still anointed the nooks and hollows.

'Look.' Luc pointed a slender finger. 'You can just see the tower.'

'Tower?'

'Yes, the house has a tower. It is a monstrosity.' He laughed bitterly.

'Don't you like it?'

'Like it?' When he looked at her, his top lip almost snarled. 'Does a convict like his prison?'

Jess shook her head. 'I don't understand.'

'I hate it.' His mouth turned down in a sulk.

'Why do you live there then?'

He was old enough, she thought, to live where he wanted. He didn't need his mother's apron strings.

'My mother,' he said, 'she is ill. She needs someone.'

Jess touched his arm in sympathy. 'I'm sorry . . . I didn't realize. Peggy just said—'

He whirled on her. 'Peggy said what?'

She looked embarrassed. 'Er . . . just that she never goes out. I told you.'

He smiled, golden eyes cold as frozen nuggets.

'And I said that was not true, did I not? She does go out, mostly at nights.'

'Why at night?'

Luc shrugged. 'She does not like to meet people,' he waved his hand in the air. 'Sometimes she walks during the

51

day . . . in the winter. She likes the winter.'

Jess shivered. She suddenly wanted the warmth of the kitchen fire, the company of the animals. Cats. Dogs. Ponies who asked no questions. No favours. She shivered, hugged herself. 'I'm going back.'

'No. Come and see the house. I want you to see it.'

She felt powerless to refuse.

He took her hand again. Rubbed it between his own.

'Your hand is cold.'

'Everything's cold.'

He put his arm round her. She stiffened, closed her eyes. *Danny . . . I'm sorry.*

'You do not mind, do you?' She heard his voice, soft, in her ear. His breath felt like a moth's wing against her cheek. The sensation seemed to be drawing her into another land, a world of forest scents and shadows.

'No,' she murmured.

Suddenly he leapt away. 'Come on,' he called. 'Race you, that will warm us up.'

She crashed through the trees after him. His long strides, taking him far beyond her, reminded her of a greyhound's grace. Leaves scattered like amber snow. Her eyes, nose, ran with moisture.

'Wait, you pig,' she shouted. 'Wait for me!'

At the end of the path she skidded to a halt. She clutched a tree trunk to steady herself. Around, the forest seemed to be asleep. A leaf fell. It settled on the toe of her boot like a wrinkled bronze butterfly.

'Luc?' she called uncertainly. Where was he? Had he disappeared as mysteriously as he had arrived earlier on, just at the very moment she had been thinking about him?

'Luc . . . ?'

He grabbed her from behind a tree. She fell. Him on top, rolling over and over in the sodden leaves. Laughing. They came to a halt. She felt his breath on her face. The smell of his skin brushed her consciousness. Helpless, giggling, she beat feebly at his shoulders, his back.

'Let me get up, Danny . . . you're squashing me!'

Her hand flew to her mouth. Suddenly she was crying helplessly. Oily tears, hot on her face. She squeezed her eyelids tight and drew a deep, sobbing breath. She spread her arms out wide on the forest floor as if she was being crucified. She felt his weight lift from her. She turned and buried her face in her arms. She felt the light touch of his hand on her head. A soft noise, a whine, from his throat. He lay beside her, his murmured words of sympathy wafting her hair.

'I'm sorry . . . ' Jess sat up. She wiped her face angrily with the sleeve of her jacket. She fumbled desperately in her pocket for a tissue.

'Here.' He handed her a grubby, rust-stained handkerchief.

'Thanks.' Jess blew her nose. The handkerchief had a dark, metallic smell. She must look awful. As if she'd been dragged screaming through a hedge backwards. 'I'm really sorry.'

He reached out and tucked her hair behind her ear. His eyes were full of bright sympathy. 'Are you all right, now?' He gently stroked her hair.

She nodded wordlessly. She sniffed. 'I'd like to tell you about Danny. I really would.'

'Please . . . ' he said.

By the time they reached Spital House, Jess had told Luc about Danny. About their time together . . . about the accident. She hadn't told him everything, though. She wasn't ready to tell him everything. Not yet.

'I know it's stupid,' Jess said, 'but I still pretend he's here. I still talk to him although I know he's gone and can never come back.'

'It was meant to be,' Luc said with such certainty that she threw him a surprised glance. 'You must believe that, Jess. It is all part of a pattern, everything is part of a pattern.'

53

'What bloody pattern?' she shouted at him angrily.

'Nature's pattern.'

She shook her head. 'Is it part of your precious pattern to feel so angry, so betrayed, so lost, so bloody stupid?'

'You are not lost, Jess,' he said simply. 'I am here now.'

He sounded so sure that she gave him another quick, startled glance.

A pair of iron gates loomed ahead. Tall, forbidding, some kind of family crest wrought like a spider in a hard, metal web in the centre of each one. A rusted padlock and chain held them together.

Jess looked through the bars. As far as she could see, a straight driveway led up to the house. It was so overgrown with brambles it was hard to tell whether there was a path there or not. Jess screwed up her eyes. The house seemed shrouded in fog. A distant chess piece. A miasma of something hovered over the turreted rooftops like a threat. She could see its tower, like a church, yet . . . less like a church than anything she had ever seen. She drew in her breath. She felt better than she'd done for ages, somehow purged. As if telling Luc had made everything all right for the time being.

'Wow!' She turned to Luc. 'It looks like a stately home or something.'

'Or something,' he said.

'It looks really creepy.'

'Creepy?'

'Yes . . . ghostly . . . like something out of one of those old horror films, you know?'

Luc shrugged. 'I have never seen a . . . horror film.'

'What . . . don't you have a TV?' Jess felt shocked. She had never known anyone who didn't have a television, or, come to think of it, anyone who had never been to school.

Luc shook his head. 'No. I do have a radio. I found it in someone's dustbin and bought batteries in the village. I do not know why they had thrown it away, it works very well.'

'Oh.' Jess didn't know what to say. 'Well, that's something.'

'Yes,' he smiled down at her. She tore her eyes away from his.

'Why do you keep the gates locked?'

He shrugged indifferently. 'I climb the wall. They have been locked for years. Ever since my grandparents died. I have not thought about unlocking them.'

'But . . . '

She looked at him, wanting to say something else. But his face was closed up.

He took her arm suddenly. 'Very well . . . you have seen it. We shall go back now.' He seemed in a hurry, as if he had realized coming here was a big mistake.

'But . . . '

'What?'

'I'd like to see it close up. You wanted to show it to me, remember?' Jess had been anxious to get back too. But now, seeing the house . . . it was drawing her like a magnet. She'd always had a curiosity about old places. Castles, derelict houses. She always wanted to see inside.

'I forgot you would have to get over the wall.'

'Don't be daft . . . ' Now it was Jess who was enticing him. 'I can climb a wall as well as you. Come on, Luc. Your mother won't mind if you bring a friend, will she?'

He seemed to draw away from her. His nostrils flared. He turned up the collar of his jacket.

He shrugged. 'I do not know . . . I have never—'

'You've never what?'

'I have never had a friend.'

Jess put her hand on his arm. She felt easier with him now. As if she had known him all her life. 'Luc . . . I'm sorry.'

He shrugged. 'It does not matter . . . now I have you.'

She saw him smile suddenly. His eyes glowed as if he had won a great victory. He'd done it on purpose. He'd made her want to go in.

'Very well,' he said. 'Let us go in.'

He sprang to the top of the wall and held out his hand. She grunted with effort as he pulled her up. A loose stone rattled to the ground. He pulled her against him, steadying her, his breath on her face. She felt the lean, hard muscles of his thighs. He let her go, jumped down the other side and held out his arms.

4

LUC

Luc watched her face as she jumped down from the wall. He held out his hands to steady her. She looked better, less pale. As if her burden was lighter. Yet he knew it was still there, that she was clinging on to her memories. He had told her that her grief was part of a pattern. What would she say when he told her exactly where *she* fitted in to that pattern?

She was staring at the house. Her confidence had ebbed away. Her initial curiosity tempered by apprehension. He could see she felt the malevolence—even from there. He was glad she was sensitive. He needed her to be.

'It is all right,' he said, teasing. 'Gollum is not really in there.'

She turned to him and smiled. 'It still looks pretty scary. Have your family really lived here for hundreds of years.'

'Yes,' he said. 'They came over from France in the eighteenth century.'

They were almost to the front door. Luc had never bothered to pull down the rampant creeper that had sealed it shut for several decades.

'I wonder why they chose a house like this . . . so far away from everybody.'

'I wonder,' he said.

He could see she was puzzled at his reply. But it would all come clear. Later. When he told her.

Jess stared upwards at the tower. She put her hand above her eyes as if to see better. The shades were, as usual, drawn against the daylight.

'Do you use it?'

'Use what?' He stroked the back of her hand. He was fascinated. The smooth, hairless paleness . . . the freckles.

The delicate bones. The hint of a blue, throbbing vein beneath the paper skin. He swallowed. She seemed unaware of his fascination.

'The tower,' she was saying.

'My mother does,' he said.

Jess turned to him, uncertainty marking her face. 'Maybe I had better get back. Your mum might be annoyed if you bring someone unexpectedly. My mother . . . '

'Yes?'

She shrugged. He saw the spark of bitterness that ignited her green eyes. 'She always thinks she needs to clean the place up before anyone comes. It's daft though, it's always spotless anyway. Like those show houses you see in magazines.'

'You do not have to worry about my mother, she does not think about that kind of thing. She leaves it up to me, and I,' he shrugged, 'I am not very good, as you will see. Anyway, my mother will probably be in bed. She often sleeps in the daytime.'

Jess threw him a look of sympathy. It felt strange . . . to have someone look at him like that.

'Is that why you do the shopping and stuff . . . because she's ill.'

'Yes . . . '

Things were moving too fast, she was asking too many questions. It was too soon. She must learn to trust him first. Unless she trusted him she would never believe him, do as he asked. 'Stay a little while, please?' He tilted his head to one side.

She gave in, half smiling at him. 'OK.'

He led her round the back. Brambles snared their progress. One caught at her leggings.

'Oh, shit!' Jess bent to extricate herself. 'They're the only pair I've got.'

'Did it scratch you?' He tried to help. Through the hole he could see red blood welling. He stared, fascinated.

'Let me . . . ' He knelt beside her, heedless of his own

58

clothes catching in the bramble's vicious claw. He held her calf in his hands. He moved the torn material aside, lowered his head . . .

She jerked away. She laughed. Embarrassed, puzzled. 'God, Luc, it's just a scratch, for goodness' sake.'

'I am sorry. I thought this was what you were supposed to do. If ever I cut myself . . . '

He felt her shrink away. 'No . . . it's fine, honestly.'

He stood up. 'I ought to clear this path, it is a mess.'

She was looking at him as if she thought he was crazy.

You are not far wrong, my little one, he thought. Not far wrong.

He opened the door that led through into the kitchen. He saw her shrink back at the smell. 'Come on, you wanted to see.' He took her elbow and propelled her firmly, almost violently, inside. He felt her reluctance, her fear. He smiled bitterly. 'As you will see, we are not used to having visitors.'

He had left his radio on. Wild rock music blared out, heavy metal sounds twanging through the air. He loved the harsh, rhythmic pulse. He remembered how he f lt the first time he had heard it. It had opened up a whole new world for him. It was as if the sounds set his spirit free. He had danced round the room, moving his body in time with the music. Up until then, the only music he had heard were ancient, scratchy, mournful violin records on his mother's old wind-up gramophone. A relic of his grandparents, acquired before his mother was born.

He went to turn it off.

'I always leave the radio on,' he explained. 'It is as if I am not really returning to an empty house.' He wondered if she knew how killing loneliness could be.

'Empty? But your mum?'

He shrugged.

He watched her as she looked round. Her eyes scanned the room. She was taking it all in. The dark green, dirty walls. The cobwebs, the old blanket thrown across the settee. She screwed up her nose at the empty cans on the table, the floor . . . the piled up bowls in the sink . . . the grease, the smell . . . the bones. Even the bundle of dried herbs and grasses hanging by the fireplace could not disguise the stink.

She turned as if to say something. She was shocked. As if she could not believe anyone could live in such squalor.

Jess seemed to change her mind about speaking. He wondered what she was going to say. Did she pity him? Did she think he was, how did she say it? Nuts?

As he watched her face, her fingers flew unconsciously to the locket at her throat. He wondered where she got it. If . . . Danny . . . had given it to her? A token of love . . . a seal on their relationship. He laughed out loud.

She turned, wide eyed, puzzled. 'What's funny?'

He shook his head. 'Nothing.' He put out his hand and picked up the locket. It was heart shaped, quite large for such a piece of jewellery. He wondered if it was given in love. The silver lay shining on his hand. He sucked in his breath. He could smell the hard, metallic smell. He had read about silver. It had special properties . . . magic properties, one of his old books told him. He felt the chain tug her skin. It was fine, weak. If he jerked it it would come off.

'Did Danny give you this?' He gazed at her face. He saw pain, sharp in her eyes.

She looked away. 'Yes.'

Suddenly he jerked the locket. The chain broke.

'Oh, God, Luc.' Her hand flew to her throat. 'You stupid twit!'

He clutched the silver. It seemed hot in his grasp. The chain dangled from his closed fist. 'You're free now,' he said. He held it up high above her head.

She jumped, trying to grab it. 'Luc, give it back. You've broken it, you stupid . . . !'

She was so close to him, she almost stepped on his feet. The whole length of her body brushed his as she tried to reach it.

60

'Luc . . . give it back!' Anger flared in her eyes.

'All the time you wear it you are tied to him, Jess,' he said.

'I *want* to be tied to him.'

'Do you . . . a dead man?'

'Give it back, Luc!'

He dropped it into her open hand. His palm seemed to itch, as if it had branded a mark on his flesh. 'Forgive me,' he said. 'That was stupid of me. I will mend it for you.'

'No, I'll do it myself. It's broken before, the locket's really too heavy for the chain.'

'You are sure?'

'Yes.' She put it in her pocket. Her face was flushed. He could feel the heat from her. 'Why did you do that, Luc? Why did you break it?'

'I wanted you to be free.'

I want you for myself . . . He just managed to stop himself from saying the words out loud. It was too soon.

Jess looked at him, still angry, but didn't say any more.

'Well?' He took off his jacket and threw it on the settee. He waved his hand. 'What do you think of Gollum Castle? You have never seen a place like this before?'

She shook her head. 'No.' She shuddered and looked round with distaste.

'I did tell you I am not a very good housekeeper,' he said.

'It's OK, really.'

The previous day's newspaper was lying on the table. Luc had been in the village shop when he saw the blaring headline. Jess picked it up.

'Oh . . . you've cut out that story about the creature.'

Luc swore under his breath. He should have got rid of the paper before she came.

'Er . . . ' he said, 'yes.'

She looked at him. 'What for?'

He shrugged. 'I am just interested in that kind of thing, that is all.'

She gave him an odd look.

'It's horrible—that poor goat.' She looked at him with shining eyes. 'I hope they catch the creature. That's why Jack came this morning . . . to ask Peggy if she'd take part in a hunt.'

Luc felt a stab of fear. He thrust his hands into the pockets of his jeans to stop them trembling. 'A hunt?' He tried to sound casual, as if his question did not really matter.

'Yes, they're going to try to capture it alive if it comes back. They reckon they'll be able to track it if it snows.'

Luc swallowed then ran his tongue around his lips. 'Have they tried before? The . . . creature has been in this area for . . . ' he shrugged, ' . . . some time.'

'I don't know,' Jess said. 'Maybe it's getting bolder now the weather is so cold. Maybe they think there's a better chance of capturing it.'

'Or killing it.'

'Yes.'

'Did Peggy say she would help?'

'Yes. She doesn't want it killed though . . . nor do I.'

Before he had time to think of a reply, her eye caught something on the floor. 'Hey,' she exclaimed. 'I didn't know you had a dog.'

She was looking at a large knuckle-bone lying on the hearth.

He picked it up and threw it into a corner. 'A stray,' he lied quickly. 'I haven't seen it for days.'

'You should have brought it to us.'

He shrugged. He wondered if she knew he was lying. He wondered if she could read things in his eyes . . . just as he could read things in hers.

'Do you want to see the rest of Gollum Castle, then?'

She looked at him. 'If you want. What about your mum . . . will she mind us tramping all over the house?'

'No,' he said. 'As long as we do not disturb her.'

'OK, then.' Her hand went to her pocket. She patted it unconsciously to make sure the locket and chain were still there. Luc could see them in his mind's eye. Lying there curled snug in her pocket. Like a serpent.

He took her down the dim corridor. The walls were lined with ancient, grimy portraits.

'My ancestors,' he explained. He sucked his palm. It still seemed to burn where the locket had lain.

Jess stopped at a picture of a young woman. 'They're really old.'

'Yes.'

She touched the picture. Her finger left a print on its dusty surface. 'Who's this? She's pretty.'

Luc felt his gorge rise. He swallowed hastily. He should have destroyed the pictures. Got rid of the faces, the bloodline. He hated them. They were like knives in his heart.

'Her name was Perrenette,' he said.

Jess's eyes were shining as she looked at him. It was all he could do not to lean forward, to touch her full mouth with his, taste her. His tongue flicked out to lick his lips. He wondered what she would do? Resist him? She couldn't keep him at bay for ever. He rubbed his sweating hands on the thighs of his jeans.

'What a lovely name,' she breathed. 'Who was she?'

He shrugged. 'Some ancient relative.'

'When was it painted? It looks so old.'

'She lived in the sixteenth century . . . in France, the Jura region.'

'Wow! You should get the pictures cleaned up. They must be worth loads of money.'

'What for?'

'Well, they're so dark and dismal . . . '

'We are a dark and dismal family,' he said bitterly.

If only you knew, my Jessica, he thought. If only you knew.

She glanced at him then moved on.

'Who's this?'

The portrait was of a man in his thirties with a fat

stomach and bright eyes. He wore brown breeches, a cream-coloured waistcoat with a white neckerchief.

'His eyes are like yours,' Jess said, looking at Luc.

'That is Pierre,' he said. 'Perrenette's brother.'

'And this?' The third painting was at the bottom of the dark stairway that led to the tower.

'Antoinette, another sister.'

'Perrenette,' she murmured. 'Pierre, Antoinette, what beautiful names.'

He snorted.

'Do you know anything about them?'

'Yes,' he took her hand, 'a lot.' He wanted desperately to tell her about them but knew it was too soon.

There were other portraits too. The last one was of a young woman; her evening dress scarlet lace. Her raven hair was piled on top of her head. Her stare seemed to bring Jess to a halt.

'Who's that?' Luc heard her sharp intake of breath.

'My mother.'

Jess looked at him. 'She's beautiful. She . . . ' Jess was staring at the amber eyes, the elegant hands resting gracefully in her lap. Luc often stood in front of the portrait, gazed at it, not believing it was really her. There was something elemental about her, as if she truly belonged to the rich, autumn landscape pictured behind her.

'She's really like you,' Jess was saying. 'Except for her dark hair.'

He snorted derisively. 'Is she?'

He took Jess's arm and led her away. He couldn't bear to look at the portraits. If it wasn't for his mother he would have taken them down and burned them long ago.

As they moved together along the corridor, his sharp ears caught more sounds from the upper floor. A creak of bedsprings, a scratching sound. His hackles rose. He glanced quickly at Jess. Surely, she must have heard it too? He cursed himself for not shutting the outer doors before he left.

'What was that?' She held her breath. Her hand grew tense in his.

'Nothing. My mother . . . she sometimes tosses and turns . . . ' he broke off, lamely. Why was he telling her this? She had got to know the truth sooner or later.

'Hadn't you better go up and see if she's OK?'

'Later,' he said.

'What's in here?' Jess stood in front of one of the doors that led off the corridor.

'Books,' he said.

She laughed as if she didn't believe him.

'Books? Is that all?' Her fingers hovered over the handle.

'Take a look if you do not believe me!'

He threw open the door with a flourish. He felt her draw close to him as a draught of cold air greeted them. She wrinkled her nose at the smell. Mould, decay . . . he was used to it. He hardly noticed it at all.

'Look,' he said, throwing his arms wide. 'I told you.'

The walls were lined with old, leather-bound books. Ragged curtains draped the windows. On the table a globe—yellowed, weird creatures drawn in its oceans. Dust lay everywhere like a covering of fine, polluted snow. On books, on furniture . . . Pennants of cobwebs joined the corners of the room like grotesque bridges of lace.

'Wonderful, is it not?'

Ignoring him, Jess went in. She walked round the room. He saw her touch a dusty statuette on the wine table . . . glance upward at the dripping crystal chandelier. Then she bent and picked the top book off a pile on the floor.

'*A Tale of Two Cities*,' she said. She wiped green mould off the leather cover with her sleeve. 'I did it for my GCSE.'

'GCSE?'

'An exam you take at school.'

'Oh.'

'Peggy told me you'd never been to school . . . is that true?' Jess looked at him sideways.

School . . . He could just imagine it. The taunts. The

65

bullying . . . anyone who was different . . . who did not even seem to belong to this world.

'Yes,' he said. 'It is true.'

'Your mother taught you at home?'

He shrugged. 'Not really . . . most things I have learned myself.' He waved his hand. 'From these . . . there are books here on almost every subject in the world.' It was true. Luc had learned everything he knew from the books. They had explained so many things to him. 'After I learned to read,' he went on, 'she left me to my own devices. Especially since—' he broke off.

'Since what?'

'Since she became ill.'

'Luc . . . can nothing be done for her? Surely a doctor could—?'

'No . . . ' he interrupted. 'A doctor could do nothing.'

Luc saw Jess shiver as if she could read his mind. He smiled inwardly. If she could really read his mind she would almost certainly run away.

She opened the book and glanced at the flyleaf. His grandfather's name was inscribed there . . . Jean Gandillon . . . he had seen it many times. She picked up another book.

'*The Strange Case of Dr Jekyll and Mr Hyde* . . . wow, creepy . . . ' She was smiling. She looked at the spine of another. '*Tales of Mystery and Imagination*. These are great, Luc.' She smiled again and looked up at him. 'Have you read all these?'

'Most of them,' he said.

'They're really old-fashioned.'

'Are they?' He shrugged. He had never thought of his books as being old-fashioned. 'Yes . . . I suppose they are. Some of them were bought by my grandfather . . . and his grandfather before him.'

'I love old books,' she said.

He waved his hand. 'You may borrow some if you wish.'

'No . . . it's OK . . . but I know where to come if I get short of something to read.'

'Yes,' he said. Then . . . 'Come on, let us get back to the kitchen.'

'Is that where you spend your time?' Jess asked. 'In that . . . kitchen?'

He nodded, shutting the door quietly. If his mother heard them, she might call out. He could not risk it. 'The rest of the house is very damp . . . hardly habitable.'

'Except the tower.'

'Yes.'

'Take me up there?'

'Now?'

'Yes, please, Luc. I'd love to see it.' She was so beautiful as she smiled her green-eyed smile at him. *Oh, my beautiful Jess—you'll love the tower. You'll really love the tower.*

'Very well,' he said. 'If you insist.'

The stairs were steep, winding. Jess walked in front of him. She placed her palm against the wall.

'It's cold,' she said. 'Damp.' She turned, looming above him. 'Oh, Luc, how do you keep warm in a place like this?'

'You do not,' he said.

They were on the first floor landing. Jess looked out of the window.

'Wow! What a view.'

He stood close behind her. Warmth came from her as she leaned against him. He put his hand on her shoulder, feeling the bones beneath his fingertips. 'Look,' he said, pointing. 'You can see the chimneys of Peggy's house.' He could smell her hair, her curiosity. He felt dizzy, disorientated. He was breathing heavily. His heart seemed to be beating a chaotic rhythm. 'I can hear your dogs barking on a clear night.'

She turned to smile at him. 'Can you?'

'Yes . . . it makes me feel you are close to me.'

She frowned slightly. 'You do say funny things.'

'Do I?'

'Yes.' She stood on tiptoe, moving against him. 'You can't see your house from there, though. Only the tops of the trees.'

'Yes,' he said. 'Although you probably could. If you knew where to look.' He rubbed his palm.

'What's wrong with your hand?' She took it, turned it over. 'There's nothing there.'

'No,' he said. It had been his imagination . . . the heat of the silver . . . the way he thought it had marked his skin.

'Shall we go on up?' Jess was asking.

He shook his head. His ears caught the sluggish movement of his mother's herb-induced sleep. His nostrils flared. He could smell her acid smell. 'Not now,' he said quickly.

'Is one of these your room, Luc?' She indicated the three sealed doors of the round landing.

'No.'

'Which is your room, then?'

'I do not have one,' he said. 'I sleep on the settee in the kitchen.'

'Oh?'

'Are you disappointed?'

She shrugged. She tossed back her hair. 'It's just that you can tell about people from their rooms. You know, posters, tapes, that kind of stuff.'

'So if I do not have a room, I do not exist. Is that right?'

She frowned. 'You're weird.'

'So you told me.'

Her glance fell away. 'I'm sorry.'

'Do you *want* to know about me, then?'

She gazed at him again. She was trying not to be curious about him. But he knew she could not help it. She *wanted* to know about him.

He grinned softly. He almost had her . . . almost.

He saw her shrug. 'You can tell me if you like. After all, I've told you about . . . about Danny, although I don't know why I did.'

68

'Why should you not tell me about him?'

'I don't know. I've never really talked to anyone about him much.'

'I am not just anyone, am I?'

She glanced at him. 'No.'

He took her hand. 'Very well,' he said, 'I will tell you about me.' In the kitchen, he took the old blanket off the settee. He brushed away layers of dust and small round globules of mud. When she sat down he sat close beside her. She sat back, drew her knees up to her chin. Her closeness aroused him again. He put his arm round her.

'Sweet Jess,' he murmured softly.

He felt her move away from him. Not physically, something inside of her drew away from his closeness.

'Luc . . . !' her laugh trembled.

She looked at him sideways. Her cheek rested on her knee. She reached a fingertip to touch his hair. Then she drew the line of his mouth. Her touch was like an eddy of dragonfly wings on his flesh. He saw a spark of invitation in her eyes. It excited him. Maddened him. He fought to keep control. Move too fast and he would scare her. His mouth watered. He bit his bottom lip, teasing it gently between his strong teeth. He ran his tongue over his lips. He had dreamt of moments like this for a long, long time. He saw Jess frown, one eyebrow creasing in puzzlement. He stroked her cheek and felt her blood warm to his touch. He could hear the throb of it, coursing through her veins. She folded herself into him.

When he lowered his head to kiss her he knew he had won.

She tasted of all the things his wildest dreams had imagined.

When he lifted his head he heard her sigh. He knew she needed him too. Needed to be reassured she still had feelings. That they did not die with her boyfriend under the wheels of the stolen motor car. He smiled into her hair.

She stirred in his arms.

'Why are you smiling?'

'Just thinking,' he said.

He kissed her ear, running his tongue round its curves. His hands sought the waistband of her leggings. If she would just . . .

'No!' She drew back suddenly. She jumped up. 'Luc, I've got to go.'

He held on to her hand. 'I am sorry, I thought—' He was panting. He swallowed noisily. His heart beat like the drumming of a hunter's hoofs. If she went now he might never find out if she . . . He would have to look for someone else . . . then it might be too late. He felt his hands curving into claws of terror.

'You thought what?'

He looked down, away from the blaze of her uncertainty. 'I thought that you . . . ' He had to be careful.

'That I what? Go on, Luc, *say* it!'

'I thought maybe you wanted to—'

'Make love to you? Is that it, Luc?'

'You seemed . . . '

'What?'

'As if you wanted to.' He lowered his eyes. 'Sorry.'

He heard her whisper. 'It's OK, it doesn't matter.'

His hair had come loose. It shrouded his face. He tossed it back. 'Yes, it does,' he said. 'I thought you wanted to make love with me . . . pretend I was Danny.'

She turned away and headed for the door. 'You're disgusting, Luc.' She flung the words over her shoulder at him.

'No!'

She's not going to tell me . . . He held his breath. *She's not going to . . .*

He was off the settee in one enormous bound. He grabbed her arm. 'Jess, I am sorry. I thought it might help.'

She shook her head. 'It won't help, nothing will help. Anyway . . . I . . . '

'You what?' Time held its breath.

'I haven't . . . me and Danny, we didn't . . . '

He breathed a sigh of relief. 'I am sorry. I assumed . . . why? Why did you and Danny not . . . I thought you loved him.'

'He wanted to . . . I was scared,' she shrugged her shoulders. 'I didn't want the commitment.'

'But?'

'I did love him. I just didn't want my relationship with Danny to take over my life. You see it all the time . . . getting pregnant at sixteen, ruining your life. I'm not stupid even if some people are.'

Luc threw back his head. His laughter echoed round the high kitchen. He pushed his hair back from his face. Then he grabbed Jess and waltzed round the room with her. Empty cans, screwed-up paper, old cartons, flew around their feet. He switched on the radio as they flew past. Radio 1 blared out. Something by Genesis . . . he recognized it straight away. ' . . . and crept right over my heart . . . '

'Luc!' She struggled in his arms. 'For God's sake . . . ' She was laughing, she couldn't help it. Her face looked flushed.

At last he let her go. She staggered back. She shook her head. 'You're as nutty as a fruit cake.' She was grinning, unable to help herself. 'Look, you idiot, I've really got to go.'

Sobering up, he held her arm. 'No . . . not yet . . . ' He held up his hands. 'I will not touch you again, I promise.'

'It's not that. I . . . ' There was something like disappointment in her eyes.

He put his hand over her mouth. Gently. The time had come . . . the time to tell her everything.

'Jess,' he said, 'be quiet a minute. Please. I am going to tell you about myself . . . my family. It will not take long.'

5

JESS

Luc left her at the edge of the forest. On the way back he had hardly spoken. She wanted him to take her hand. He didn't. He just walked beside her, his long legs taking him now and then ahead of her. He didn't even look her in the eye. He just waited for her to catch up without a word. She knew he was anxious to be rid of her.

Jess remembered the feel of his lips. The hand curving her waist. The spell he cast. She must be going crazy, really going crazy.

He had been going to tell her about his life. The strange, solitary existence. He had seemed anxious she should know. As if telling her might make it bearable.

Then it had come . . . the noise, the scream, the cry of terror and frustration.

It had frozen them both into silence. Hours later, the memory still chilled.

'Luc . . . ?' Her heart had drummed with fright. 'What on earth . . . ?' She had covered her ears. 'Luc . . . for God's sake!'

He had snarled. She had looked at him and he was snarling. His generous mouth curled upwards. Those lips that had tasted hers trembled over his teeth. His eyes glowed with fear and anger. He had leapt up, flung himself out of the room.

'Stay here, Jess. Do not move . . . ' he shouted.

The sound of his footsteps echoed up the winding stair. Doors slammed . . . two. Feet drumming another flight, fading away into the clouds. The sound had stopped, suddenly. Cut off, as if the screamer had been beheaded.

In a while he came back. Blood scored his cheek—a long

scratch from eye socket to jawbone. He took her arm roughly. 'Jess, you must go home.'

'Luc, what was it? What's happened?'

'It is her . . . she is really sick. I am sorry if it scared you.' He seemed calm now in the face of her terror.

'Luc, you really should get a doctor.'

'No . . . I make her an infusion of herbs from the forest. It helps her sleep. She will be all right.'

They were outside by now. He was propelling her down the side path, heedless now of the brambles that set snares to prevent them leaving.

'But, Luc, your cheek?'

She had stopped, reached up, touched the ooze. He had caught her hand in his own. Watched her eyes as he wiped his blood from her fingertips. She saw his pupils dilate, the gold-flecked irises twist and turn.

'It's nothing,' he whispered. 'Nothing.' But his eyes were full of pain.

'Luc, you were going to tell me—'

'It can wait. Another day or two will do no harm.'

He had hustled her away from Spital House. She didn't even have a chance to look back. What would she have seen? A mad woman's crazy face looking from the tower window. Matted hair, staring eyes? Luc's blood beneath her fingernails?

Peggy frowned when Jess told her what happened. She shook her head. 'I know they're an odd lot . . . but, I don't know, Jess. Maybe I should go there and see if I can help.'

'Yes,' said Jess. 'How can someone his age cope with a sick woman on his own? Honestly, Peggy . . . he knows nothing about the real world. Everything he knows comes from a load of ancient books and a crackly old radio . . . Oh, and he gets newspapers sometimes, but they don't tell you about the real world, do they?'

'Some people think they do. But in fact they give a very

73

distorted view of life . . . that's why I never read them. And to someone like Luc, living alone,' Peggy shrugged. 'Who knows what fantasies fester in his mind?'

'He does say some very strange things. You were right when you said he seemed like a child. Yet in some ways he's like a wise old man . . . poor Luc.' Jess felt helpless.

'Maybe I should phone the doctor?'

Jess shook her head. 'I suggested that. He said he makes his mother medicine from stuff he gathers in the forest.'

Peggy sighed. 'That's probably just as good as anything a doctor could provide . . . as long as he knows what he's doing.'

'Well, it's not making her any better. I reckon she's been ill for years. Ever since he was a little boy.'

'Are you seeing him again?'

Jess shook her head. 'I don't know . . . I hope so,' she added as an afterthought.

Jess sat up in bed. A wand of moonshine cast spells across her pillow. There was a bright, quicksilver shaft across the floor. The moon was waxing, clear and bright like a slowly expanding florin. She could make out its half-face tonight.

She drew her knees to her chin. The old woolly cardigan Peggy had lent her was drawn tight across her breasts. She wondered where the forest beast was tonight. Was it stalking some unsuspecting deer? Scratching around someone's barn? Stupid, but she hoped it had gone far away. She hoped it was free. She imagined it running through the forest, over moorland, eyes scanning moonlit heathlands. They were planning to hunt it down. Everything was ready. The men . . . the guns . . . dogs.

She shuddered. Why should she care anyway? The beast had attacked, killed, it had to be stopped. 'There's little likelihood of capturing it alive,' Jack Stride had said, still at the farm, when she'd arrived home. She hadn't mentioned the business with Luc until she and Peggy were on their own. 'It's obviously pretty desperate,' Jack had gone on. 'Coming so close. It could be a child next.'

Jess listened to the darkness. Everything was quiet. Then it came, someone's dog . . . howling in the distance, echoing through the still night air like a warning. Strangely, though, the kennel dogs stayed silent. Maybe only she could hear it? Maybe it was calling out to her?

Jess thought about Luc. That weird and terrible noise from the tower. She must be crazy to have anything to do with him. What was up there, for God's sake? Was his mother really a lunatic? Locked up in a tower away from sanity? Or was she just in terrible pain? Was there any medicine in the world that would silence such agony?

Jess had been desperate to know. She had begged him to explain.

'Another time,' he'd said. 'I will tell you another time.' He was scared, she could tell. Scared and angry . . . His anger frightened her. Jess had always been scared of anger. Her father's, a teacher at school who'd gone barmy once . . . Danny's . . . her own. Luc's whole body had been tense. Like an animal, nostrils flaring, eyes blazing . . . his hair, a lion's tawny mane.

She saw his hands trembled. The hands that had trembled as they touched her. She remembered the way he had whispered her name, Jess . . . Jess . . . a sound like distant breezes.

Jess ran her tongue over her lips. It was still there—the taste of him. As if he had marked her as his own.

Jess sighed and buried her face in her knees.

I'm going crazy . . . I'm really going crazy . . . I've suspected it for ages . . . now I'm sure.

She lay down, burying her face in the pillow to shut out the moonlit turmoil of her memory.

It wasn't until Jess awoke, trembling, that she realized she'd even been asleep.

It had all seemed so real. Running. Bracken, sharp spines of furze reached out for her naked legs. Breath . . . desperate gasps. They were getting closer. People with guns . . . dogs . . . Vehicle engines roared. She could smell the sharp, acrid smell of her own terror. She had stayed ahead of them easily at first. Crossing streams, weaving in and out of trees. Senses alert. A hawk, way above, screamed a warning. It had been raining, the fine, sharp scents crashing into her senses. Everything glistened, showers of fairy dust from each leaf, each flower. Swiftly she crossed the forest clearing . . . sniffing . . . smells of two people . . . food . . . lingered on the air.

The baying of dogs sent new fear rocketing through her veins. The hunters had left their vehicles and were on foot. Plunging like an army of giants. She had swerved between the trees, over logs, taking the path of streams. Exhausted now, hair matted with sweat, arms, legs . . . flesh torn and bloodied. Gaining . . . gaining . . . she could smell hot breath, the excitement of the dogs . . . the sweat of the men . . . the click of the shotgun trigger was like thunder . . . Then there was something ahead of her, blocking the path. A figure . . . long golden hair . . . golden eyes . . .

Then she was lying in bed, staring into the echoing darkness, breath stilled. The men, the guns . . . Luc . . . ?

There was a noise outside, a scrabbling rat-sound against the window. The squeak of claws made a crazy devil's tune against the glass. She heard a low, menacing growl like a far off hint of madness. Jess froze. On the back of her neck, hackles rose in feral warning. She heard a pig-snuffling around the frame. She wanted to call out but something imprisoned her in a cage of terror. Her mouth opened, nothing came out. She felt her heart beat a wild tune of panic.

And then, suddenly . . . nothing. Only an owl, hoo hoo, through the bitter midnight air and the dull drone of aeroplane engines high up above the clouds.

She sat up with a start, eyes wide. The sky was a shroud of coal, not a single star. Jess rubbed her eyes, shivered. A dream . . . a chase . . . something outside . . . God, she really was going mad.

Loud as thunder, a shot barked out, echoing across the valley.

Her stomach knotted. 'Peggy!'

Jess leapt out of bed. She grabbed her coat, dragged it on over the old T-shirt she wore in bed. She stuffed her feet into fluffy slippers.

The light was on in the kitchen. A cold blast of air blew in from the wide-open back door.

'Peggy!' Jess screamed from the threshold.

'I'm out here!'

Peggy was standing by the feedstore, shotgun still smoking. Snow danced in the bright shafts from the outside lamp. She wore only a pair of man's pyjamas, slippered feet curled against the bitter cold.

'What was it?'

'I'm not sure. The beast I think. Didn't you hear the dogs?'

I heard dogs but they were chasing my dream.

'No . . . at least . . . I thought I was dreaming.'

'I can assure you, you weren't.'

'Peggy, come in, you'll die.'

But Peggy ignored her. She walked around the yard. 'Get the torch will you, Jess?'

Jess got the flashlight from the window shelf. She grabbed a scarf and wrapped it over her head. She grabbed a coat for Peggy.

Outside it was snowing heavily now. Bone-chilling winds whistled round the outbuildings, down over the valley like a banshee's lament.

'Thanks.' Peggy put the safety catch on the gun and propped it up against the wall. She thrust her arms into the coat. 'Let's take a look round the back.'

Peggy picked up the gun and strode round to the rear of

the house. The torchlight caught the eyes of old Barney, the ram, wide with fear. He was huddled in the corner under a hawthorn tree. He bleated softly.

The torch beam swung in a wide arc. A few yards away something red huddled in the snow.

'Oh, God . . . !' Peggy suddenly switched off the light.

Jess caught the back of her coat. 'What . . . ?' Her voice was shrill against the howling wind. 'Peggy . . . what?'

'Go in, Jess,' Peggy shouted.

'No, Peggy, tell me!' Jess realized she was shaking all over.

Peggy took her arm. 'I'm afraid it's got the poor old ewe.'

Jess's hand flew to her mouth. 'Oh, no . . . poor thing!'

'Jess, go in . . . I just want to make sure she's dead. If she isn't I'll have to destroy her . . . please go in, Jess, there's nothing you can do.'

Jess stumbled back indoors. Icy tears streamed down her numbed cheeks. She threw off her scarf then went to stir up the fire. She thrust the poker in angrily. She wiped her hand across her face.

The door opened and Peggy came in. She slammed it shut against the wind. She stamped the snow off her slippers and shrugged off her coat furiously.

Jess jumped to her feet. 'Is it dead?'

'Yes.' Peggy sounded heartbroken. 'Damn it to bloody hell . . . why didn't I put them in the barn with the others.'

'You weren't to know.'

Peggy sat down in her chair. 'No, but I should have damn well been more cautious.' She sighed. 'At least the animal went for her throat . . . poor old thing . . . what a way to go. It had started to drag her off. God knows what size it is.'

Jess sniffed and pulled herself together. 'You'd better tell the police.'

'Yep . . . in the morning will do. There's nothing we can do now. It won't come back . . . it's got its supper for tonight.'

* * *

78

In the morning, Jess saw what Peggy meant. The whole back leg of the ewe had been torn off. She turned away. The sight of the mangled and bloody corpse made her want to throw up. She waved her arms and shouted angrily at the black and sinister crows circling overhead. The sheep's eyes were open. A bloodied trail of snow showed where the creature had dragged the hind leg across the grass towards the hedge. It must have jumped it for there the trail ended.

'Poor thing,' Jess murmured. She wiped her eyes with the back of her gloved hand.

Head down, she came into the feedstore. Peggy put an arm across her shoulders. 'It's no good getting upset, Jess.'

Jess managed a wan smile. 'I know. I just hate this kind of thing, that's all.'

'I've phoned Jack. He'll take the carcass to the hunt kennels . . . no good letting it go to waste. I didn't think I'd let our dogs have it, though.'

Jess shuddered. 'No, I don't think I could have stood that.'

'It's got a den in the forest,' Peggy said to Jack when he arrived. 'There's no doubt about it. It's probably holed up somewhere for the winter.'

'You say you took a pot shot,' said Jack. 'Think you might have wounded it?'

'No, it was more to scare it off. Anyway, I hope not. A wounded big cat's more dangerous than a healthy one.'

'Do you really think that's what it is?' asked Jess.

'Can't see what else it *can* be.'

Suddenly, Jess's dream-sounds came flashing back.

'Peggy, I heard something outside my window, I'm sure I did.'

'What sort of thing?'

'Noises, scratching . . . like something was trying to get in. I suppose I could have been dreaming.'

'You probably were. I doubt a wild animal would try to get in the house.'

Jess shivered. 'God, I hope not.'

The outside phone bell suddenly began to ring.

'I'll get it,' Jess said.

It was her mother. She had the knack of ringing at the worst possible time.

'What do you want, Mum?'

Her mother laughed. 'What do I want? I want to know how you are, Jess. You haven't phoned.'

'I'm sorry, Mum. I've been busy.'

'I spoke to Peg yesterday. She tells me you've made a friend.'

'A friend?'

'A neighbour's son.'

'Oh . . . Luc, yes.' Jess could tell her mother was pleased. Someone to replace Danny? Just what her parents wanted. As long as he was respectable, of course.

'What's he like?'

'Luc . . . oh, he's . . . '

He's weird, Mother, you'd hate him. He's got this really long hair and wears a leather jacket. He's got hypnotic, amber-coloured eyes and a mad mother locked in the attic . . . and he wants to make love to me. And you know something, I want him too . . . I really want him to . . .

' . . . he's . . . er . . . nice,' Jess said vaguely, her mind still on the events of the night . . . the bloodied corpse in the snow.

'That's good, darling. What does he do?'

'Do?'

Oh, do—you mean has he got a good job with good prospects . . .?

'Yes, does he work?'

No . . . he lives in this old house in the forest and gathers herbs to help his mother sleep.

'Er . . . I don't know what he does. Is it important?'

'No, of course not, darling. By the way, I saw that girl yesterday.'

'What girl?'

'The one from the paper shop.'

Jess's heart went cold. 'Oh . . . ? So what?' *Shut up, Mum. Please shut up.*

Jess could imagine her mother shrugging. 'Nothing . . . just that she had the baby with her. A dark-haired little thing it is.'

'How interesting.'

'Jess . . . I—' her mother began.

'Mum, I don't really want to be reminded of it, thanks very much.'

'I'm sorry.'

'I know . . . I know . . . I have to face the truth. Well, I am facing the truth, Mum, that's why I'm here, aren't I?'

'Yes.'

Jess swallowed. Her breath constricted in her throat. *Why did you have to remind me, Mum? I was getting over it . . . I was really getting over it.*

'Mum, I've got to go.'

'Now you're upset. Why can't I keep my big mouth shut?'

'It's OK, it doesn't matter. I'll speak to you soon, OK? I've got to go and do my chores, Peggy's waiting.'

'Chores?'

'Yes, feeding the horses, dogs, donkey, elephants. The kind of stuff you do at a place like this.'

Her mother chose to ignore the sarcasm. 'We've been reading about that beast that's killing all the animals.'

'Yes.' Jess felt a sudden compulsion to tell her mother what had happened last night. She sighed heavily. There was no point. Her mother would only panic . . . demand that Jess went home immediately.

'You'll be careful, won't you, Jess.'

Jess sighed. 'Yes, Mum . . . Mum?' She hadn't meant to upset her. It had been hard for everyone, Mum especially. She always took the troubles of the world upon her shoulders.

'Yes?'

'I'm sorry . . . the way I spoke . . . I didn't mean . . . ' She imagined her mother blinking back tears. Stupid . . . suddenly she felt like crying too.

'It's all right, Jess. Just take care.'

'I will. You too.'

Jess slammed down the receiver. She ran her hands through her hair. *Damn, damn, damn . . .*

Jess stomped around the kitchen. *So her mother had seen Charlene's baby. So what's new? So what if it's got dark hair and dark blue eyes and . . .* Jess bit her lip. When Emma had first told her it had all become clear. Charlene's absence. 'She's gone to stay with her mother for a while,' Charlene's father told Emma when she went in the shop. Jess remembered how Charlene had lurked at the back of the chapel at Danny's funeral. How she disappeared so quickly at the end. She hadn't even stayed to see the coffin lowered. Jess remembered the swing of the loose black coat— Charlene's blonde hair covered by a scarf.

You might have guessed he'd be two-timing you, Jess . . . you stupid fool. He told you he'd had a lot of girlfriends. What made you think you were so special? That you were the one . . . the only one.

She wouldn't cry . . . she wouldn't be a wimp.

Outside, Peggy had boiled a kettle of water in the feedstore. She was pouring it over the outside tap. Clouds of steam rose in the sharp, bright air. The blue sky dazzled against the snowy landscape.

'Where's Jack?'

'He's taken the carcass down to the kennels.'

Jess was glad she hadn't been there to see it go.

'Who was on the phone?'

'Mum.'

'Oh dear, she phoned yesterday, I forgot to tell you. Did you tell her about last night?'

82

'You're joking . . . she'd have thrown a wobbly . . . demanded I go home.'

'I'm sorry if this has upset you, Jess.'

Jess shrugged. 'I'm OK, really. I must be getting better. I just feel angry, that's all.'

'So do I, angry at myself.'

'Oh, Peggy, it wasn't your fault.'

'Jack's coming back later with the RSPCA bloke . . . we're going to try to follow the tracks.'

Jess drew in a deep breath of sharp air. It was crazy but something made her hope they didn't catch it. She swallowed. 'You don't expect me to come, do you?'

'Of course not, dear girl. I don't expect you to do anything, you know that.'

'Yes, I'm sorry.'

But Peggy must have seen something in her eyes. 'Jess, what's wrong?' Peggy put a hand on her arm.

'I just hate the thought of it being killed . . . of anything else being killed.' She shook her head. 'There's so much death.'

'I know, I'm sorry. I promise you we'll take it alive if we can.'

'If you catch it, will you keep it here?'

Peggy shrugged. 'I don't know. I'm not equipped for big cats.'

'Or whatever else it might be.'

'Yes.'

The tap was running at last. Jess went to get a bucket and waited for it to fill. 'I'll see to the horses.'

She lugged the bucket of water to the gate. She stood a minute. The sight of the snow-covered landscape almost took away her breath. Everything was made soft, the forest trees were white whale humps against the stark bright blue of the clear morning sky. Even a spider's web woven between the strands of barbed wire was a filigree of bleached lace.

Suddenly the nightmare flashed. A creature, bleeding . . .

the sound of dogs . . . Jess shook her head to switch off the image.

Jess climbed the gate and went to break the ice on the pony's trough. Snow was piled high on one side where the wind had blown across the valley. Jess bent down. There was a footprint in the mud round the sheltered side. Big . . . quite clear . . . pads and claws. She felt her stomach churn. The wind seemed to freeze her bones. She heard again the scratching at her window . . . claws against glass . . .

'Have you found something?' Peggy's voice came from another planet.

Jess hastily kicked snow over the paw print. She drew an icy breath. 'No, nothing.'

Why did I do that? Why on earth . . . I must be a real nut.

Peggy was beside her. 'Here, I'll break the ice. Could you let the dogs out into their runs?'

Peggy was staring at her.

'Er . . . yeah . . . sure.'

Jess stuffed her hands into her pockets.

'Are you sure you're OK?' Peggy was frowning at her.

Jess managed a grin. 'I'm fine, honestly. I had a row with Mum, that's all,'

'Oh . . . ' Peggy gave a half smile. 'What about this time?'

'She told me she'd seen that girl . . . the one who had Danny's baby.' Jess turned, eyes wide and shining into the wind. 'Did I tell you about this girl who had Danny's baby?'

She felt Peggy's hand on her shoulder. 'No . . . you didn't tell me.'

Jess swung round to face her. 'Well, she did. He was going out with her the same time as he was going with me. You know that man you were married to . . . the bastard . . . ? Well, surprise, surprise, Danny was a bastard too.'

Peggy's face was full of sympathy. 'Oh, Jess, I'm so sorry.'

Jess laughed bitterly. 'You know, being here . . . it's working. I really think I'm getting over it, Peggy.' She thrust her hands into her coat pockets. 'I just feel angry now . . . so angry I could scream.'

'Good for you, Jess. Anger is one of the best cures I know.'

'I wish Mum hadn't mentioned it, that's all.'

'Your mother never was the soul of discretion.'

'You're not kidding.' Jess fiddled with her glove.

'That girl . . . she lives near you?'

Jess nodded wordlessly.

'Well then, you can't avoid her for ever,' Peggy said gently. 'She's going to be there when you get back.'

'Yes.'

'Why don't you come with us this morning, it'll take your mind off things?'

Jess shook her head. 'No.'

'Well . . . ' As usual, Peggy understood. 'If you do decide to, maybe your friend Luc would like to help? He must know the forest like the back of his hand.'

Jess thought a minute. 'Yes, he does. Maybe I'll go and tell him what happened last night. He might have some ideas. Do you think it's OK? The beast isn't likely to be around in daylight, is it?'

'I shouldn't think so. Are you sure you want to go on your own though?'

'Yes,' said Jess. 'I'm not scared.'

Jess trudged down the hill. In some places the snow almost came over the top of her boots. She hitched her bag up on her shoulder. Inside were two jars of home-made chutney and a cake Peggy had insisted she take for Luc's mother.

'And if there's anything else she needs, tell Luc he only has to ask.'

'I feel like Red Riding Hood,' Jess called as she waved goodbye.

At the forest edge Jess hesitated. Inside was a fairyland of misty grey. Snow hung from every twig, every branch. The bracken was bent double, russet fronds sticking out like traps set for unwary travellers. Up in the branches of a high oak, a lone rook caw-cawed into the silence. The only other sound, the squeak of Jess's boots on the snow, the dull thud now and then as a branch shed its heavy load.

Jess took a deep breath. She loved the forest and thought somehow that it knew.

She plodded on, slipping now and then on the rutted path that led to Spital House.

At the fork, Jess stopped to take a breath. Although the forest air was bitterly cold and no shafts of sunlight penetrated the thick covering of trees, she was sweating beneath her thick coat. She took off her gloves and stuffed them into her bag. She took another deep breath . . .

As Jess turned to head along the path towards Spital House she noticed movement. A few yards along the opposite track a small avalanche of snow fell from a branch. Then another . . . another . . . something was moving through the trees . . .

She drew in her breath. Maybe it was a deer . . . a wild pony . . . *the creature*? Suddenly a dark figure emerged. It brushed snow from its clothes, then began walking towards her, head down.

Jess's sharp intake of breath seemed to fill the air. The figure lifted its head swiftly, like a startled animal. Jess could see it was a woman. She was tall and slender. She wore a long, black coat . . . a black scarf covered her head . . . her face. She carried something in her hand but Jess could not make out what it was.

Jess started forwards, towards her. The figure's hand flew upwards, shielding her face. For a moment Jess imagined she saw a pair of eyes, glowing through the flimsy fabric of the scarf. They stared at her, unblinking, fixing her to the place where she stood as steadfastly as if she was chained. Then, abruptly, the figure turned swiftly and in a flurry of black and white, disappeared into the trees, dislodging snow as she went. Jess heard the headlong flight, the crack and snap of low branches and undergrowth . . . the sound fading away into the snowy distance. Then only silence remained.

'Hey!' Jess called out. 'Come back . . . please!' Her voice echoed through the heavy trees and disappeared into nothingness. Her hand flew to her mouth. She felt disappointed, bereft . . . just as she had that first time Luc flew from her sight.

'Oh . . . ' Jess shrugged, her hands fell to her sides.

Then Luc slid beside her.

Her hand flew again to her throat. She laughed hysterically. 'Oh . . . you made me jump. I saw . . . ' she pointed.

'What . . . ?' He put his arm round her as if he possessed her already.

'Someone . . . a woman . . . '

He frowned. 'A rambler, perhaps?'

Jess shook her head. 'No . . . I think . . . '

'What?' He was frowning at her, his eyes dark.

She drew a deep breath. 'I think it was your mother.'

6

LUC

Luc watched her face as she spoke to him. She was beautiful. He had dreamed of someone like her so often and now she was here. He could still hardly believe it. Her cheeks were flushed, eyes bright as fire-sparks. Beads of perspiration were like crystals on her forehead. Sweet tendrils of hair crept out from her woolly hat. He imagined its chestnut tumble. She was like a painting in one of his books. A girl . . . a castle . . . a beast . . . she had saved the beast with a kiss . . . turned it into a handsome man. That was it—'Beauty and the Beast'. It had been his favourite fairy tale. He remembered sitting on his grandmother's knee as she read it to him. It seemed so long ago . . . another life.

Jess was saying something about his mother.

'Luc . . . are you listening to me?'

'What?' His eyes washed over her. 'I am sorry . . . what did you say?'

'Luc . . . I think I saw your mother.'

He frowned. 'My mother . . . ?'

Last night, when he got back, he realized she had gone out. He had not known she had stayed out all night. He drew a breath.

'There,' he said, trying to sound calm, 'I told you she did not stay in the house all the time . . . that village gossip. None of it is true. She loves the forest, she often gathers wild mushrooms and the herbs that help her sleep.'

'She ran away.' Jess sounded disappointed.

'Like me,' Luc said. 'She is very shy and she would not expect to meet anyone on a day like this . . . you startled her, I expect.'

Jess was looking at him. A slight frown creased her brow.

Did she believe what he was telling her? If not, she would wonder why he lied to her. He must explain everything to her soon. Beg her to help him before it was too late.

'I was coming to see you.' Jess indicated the bag on her shoulder. 'Peggy sent some things for your mother. She must be a bit better if she's out walking.'

Luc almost smiled at her sweet innocence. 'Yes . . . ' he said, thinking another small lie would do no harm. 'Today she is a bit better.' He lifted his arm from her shoulders and took her hand. 'Come home with me, Jess. I have something I want to tell you.'

'There's something I've got to tell you, too . . . that creature . . . it came last night.'

He felt an icicle of fear twist in his heart. 'Came . . . ? Where?'

'To Peggy's . . . it killed the poor old ewe . . . oh, Luc . . . it was awful.'

He stopped and took hold of her arms in a sudden, fierce grip. 'But you . . . you are all right?'

'Yes, of course, although I did think I heard something outside my window. Peggy said a wild animal wouldn't try to get in. I was probably having a nightmare.'

Luc groaned. It was the worst of *his* nightmares. That something should happen to Jess.

'I am sorry about the ewe . . . it was a pet, no?'

Jess nodded. Her eyes were sad. He felt her hand grip his. She shivered. 'Come on, let us walk, it will warm us up a bit.'

They trudged along the footpath. She held his hand tightly. He looked down at the slender fingers entwined in his. He slowed his footsteps.

'What's wrong?'

He sighed. 'Nothing, I just . . . '

She smiled at him. 'What?'

'I just suddenly wanted us to be here, like this, for ever. Not go back to the house. Just to stay in the forest together for the rest of our lives.'

Jess laughed. 'You are funny, Luc. Anyway, we'd die of exposure.'

He grinned. 'I would keep you warm.' He put his arm across her shoulders and hugged her close.

'Your mum couldn't have come this way,' Jess remarked. 'There's only your footprints.'

'She has her own secret paths,' he told her. 'Remember we have lived in the forest all our lives. We know it like no other.'

'Yes.'

'Besides,' he added. 'She has a special place she likes to visit. A kind of a hide-away?'

'A hide-away?' Jess exclaimed.

'Yes. You know . . . a place to be quiet, to be safe. Those caves—remember I told you? She likes to go there.'

They walked in silence. Once or twice she slipped. He held on to her tightly, afraid she would fall.

'They're hoping to track the animal down,' Jess said suddenly.

Luc's heart thudded with fear. 'They . . . who are they?'

'Peggy and Jack Stride. And someone from the RSPCA. They want to try to take it alive. Peggy wondered if you might help as you know the forest so well?'

Luc shook his head. 'No, I . . . ' he swallowed, then glanced at her. He shrugged. 'I could not.'

She seemed to accept his answer.

The house was sinister in the snow-light. The tower stark, black against the bright morning sky. But to her it must have looked beautiful. He heard her gasp.

'Luc, it looks like an ice castle.'

A castle . . . The beast's castle . . .?

He heard her giggle. 'Something out of Disneyworld.'

He had read about Disneyworld in the newspapers. A fantasy land . . . a place where your dreams can come true.

There were tracks, footprints around the wall. The snow

was scuffed into little piles, muddied and dirty. He climbed over swiftly and held his arms out for her. His anxiety was deepening. He imagined he could hear the sound of hunters. Men with guns. They might come to the house. He had to tell her now . . . today . . . before he lost courage.

She jumped down into his arms. He felt her hot against him. He bent and gave her a quick, wild kiss. 'I love you, Jess,' he said.

He heard her sharply indrawn breath. 'You're crazy. You don't even know me.'

'But of course I know you.' He was hurrying her now, his arm across her shoulders. 'You have told me the secrets of your soul.'

'Not all of them,' she said mysteriously. 'Just because I told you some things about Danny.'

He noticed she was almost smiling. It was the first time she had said the boy's name without looking sad.

'Oh,' he said, teasing her, 'I know more than that. I know a lot more than that.'

Indoors the fire was blazing. There was a trail of mud and snow across the kitchen floor. Luc took her bag and laid it on the table. He helped her off with her coat.

'It's OK,' she said. 'I can manage.' She pulled off her hat. The chestnut tumble of her hair was just as he remembered.

'I am sorry.' Luc hung his head like a child. She laughed and pretended to punch his arm.

'It's OK. It just seems funny . . . boys don't do things like that nowadays.'

He was puzzled. 'Is it not good manners, then, to help a lady with her coat?'

He must have looked hurt.

'I'm sorry,' she blurted. 'I didn't mean to laugh at you.' She stood in front of the fire, rubbing her hands together. 'It's those old books you read . . . I really will have to get you some more up-to-date ones.'

The radio was on, blasting metal into the silence. He'd tried to clear up. He had piled up the old newspapers, the rubbish into a corner behind the settee. He saw her wrinkle her nose against the smell.

'It's really dark and gloomy in here.'

'Is it?'

He was so used to shutting out daylight he hardly noticed. He went and drew back the tattered curtains. It made hardly any difference. The light barely penetrated the thick layer of grime on the glass.

Luc lit the lamp and set it on the table.

'Don't you have electricity?' Jess asked, turning her back to the fire. She arched her spine and stretched languorously towards the heat. He saw the outline of her breasts under her sweatshirt. He dropped his eyes quickly.

He drew a deep breath to calm himself. 'No.'

She suddenly frowned. 'Yuk . . . what's that?' She was staring at the old butcher's block table in the corner. There were pools of clotting blood, gobbets of fat and gristle. A bloodstained cleaver lay on the draining board. He swore under his breath and grabbed a stained cloth from the sink. He moved aside the basket of wild mushrooms and herbs that lay beside the mess on the table.

'My mother must have prepared a meal,' he explained.

'You don't do the cooking as well then?' said Jess.

He shrugged. 'Quite often she will prepare a meal if I am out. She likes to gather food from the forest . . . I prefer to open tins.'

'Me too,' said Jess with a grin.

He ran the cloth under the tap. 'She probably heard us coming and has gone to her room.'

He sat on the settee and pulled her down beside him.

'What was it you wanted to tell me, Luc?' She looked at him so innocently. He touched her hair, then leaned his head against the back of the settee. He closed his eyes and sighed.

He could feel her looking at him, waiting for him to

speak. Then she put her arms around him, nestled her head beneath his chin. He felt a sudden, strange peace. He put his hands on her shoulders then round her back. He heard her sigh. He nuzzled his face into her neck. She was here. With him. Suddenly there seemed no urgency. Nothing else mattered.

'Well,' she murmured, 'aren't you going to tell me?'

He sighed again. 'Yes.' The fire still blazed. She looked at him wide-eyed, trusting. It was almost more than he could bear. She kindled something in him. A desire to live. A desire to be done with all this . . . to be . . . for God's sake . . . normal.

'I wanted to tell you about my family,' he began. 'My ancestors . . . ' he hesitated.

'Yes,' she said. 'Go on.'

'They have a strange history.'

She sat up, her hand still on his leg. 'Yeah . . . ? What . . . skeletons in the cupboard and all that?'

'Something like that,' he said.

She grinned. 'Great, go on.'

He leaned towards her, his hand on her knee. 'Jess, you must believe what I am going to tell you. If you do not believe me it will not be any good. You have to do it of your own free will.'

'Do what?' Suspicion ignited.

He lowered his gaze. Her fingers were twisting her locket. He was glad . . . very glad . . . she had mended it.

He sighed. 'Jess, I must start at the beginning.'

'OK, I'm sorry.'

'As I said, the Gandillon's have a strange history. They lived in France, Franche-Comté, the region in the shadow of the forested Jura mountains, rising west to Lake Leman and the Swiss Alps.'

He saw Jess relax, listening now, her beautiful face glowing in the firelight. He leaned forward, his elbows on his knees.

'The people in the portraits,' she said.

'Yes. Antoinette Gandillon, the eldest, was a beautiful woman. She lived in a large house. The family were wealthy. They were farmers and most of the village peasants were employed to work their land. She lived with her brother Pierre and his son George. Their sister Perrenette lived in the house too. Pierre's wife had died of the plague when George was three.'

'How do you know so much about them?'

'My mother told me. The family history has been passed down from generation to generation. And also it is written down, in many books about . . . about people with strange histories.'

'You mean myths and legends, that kind of stuff?'

'Yes, except the Gandillons are real . . . the stories about them are all true.'

'I see.'

'Perrenette was very strange,' he went on. 'She had given birth to a child and had not told anyone who the father was. After that, the family kept her locked up. Once though, she escaped. She wandered the forest for days before she was found.'

Luc reached out and took Jess's hand in his own. He turned it over, feeling the bird-bones. 'You are so thin,' he said absently.

She shrugged. 'I didn't each much for ages.'

'Danny?'

She nodded wordlessly. He raised her fingers to his face. Letting them rest there while he went on with the story.

'One day,' he said, 'a village child was murdered. Torn to pieces. It was the latest in a long, long line of mysterious killings. The child's brother was climbing a tree and witnessed the whole thing. He tried to defend his little sister but was fatally wounded in the attempt. He was able to tell the story before he died. He had seen a tail-less wolf with human hands kill the child. A group of peasants came upon Perrenette near the place the child was found. Since Perrenette had escaped that time, the family had been unable to keep her indoors. She hated the confines of the house. They had tried to lock her in but she would scream and shout, tearing at herself with long fingernails. She had attacked them all, biting and scratching . . . '

Beside him, Jess shivered. She withdrew her hand, sticking it into the pocket of her jeans.

Luc thought a minute. He must not frighten her. There might never be another chance.

'Eventually, they had given Perrenette a wooden shack in the grounds,' he went on. 'It was the only way she would keep quiet. She used to roam the forest at night, howling and calling out. That day,' Luc said, 'the day the child was attacked . . . the peasants killed her.'

A small cry escaped Jess's throat. 'Oh God . . . how terrible. Surely she wouldn't have done a thing like that?'

Luc shrugged. 'The peasants knew the family had a strange sister they kept locked up. Rumours had been circulating and woodmen had heard noises in the forest. Apparently Perrenette looked odd. She had wild golden hair and strode about in men's clothes.'

'That didn't make her mad.'

He shrugged again. 'You know how village people distrust anyone who is different . . . times have not changed.'

'No—I suppose not.'

She leaned forward eagerly. 'What happened then, Luc?'

'All the other members of the family were arrested. They were accused of being werewolves . . . or *loups-garoux*.'

Jess gasped. 'You've got to be joking?'

He shook his head. 'The peasants had been losing their livestock . . . they were looking for a scapegoat.'

'Poor things,' Jess murmured.

'Antoinette was not only accused of being a werewolf but a witch too. So was Pierre. They were tortured. Later, they both confessed. Pierre told his torturers he dressed in wolfskins and killed sheep and cattle. Perrenette, he said, had killed many children in the same guise. George, his son,

95

was dragged in and tortured. He confessed to making an ointment of poisonous herbs that turned them into wolves. All three were burned at the stake.'

'Oh no!' Jess exclaimed. 'Oh God, Luc. Your poor family. I expect if they were tortured they would have said *anything* to make their torturers stop.' She stared at him. 'What happened to Perrenette's child?'

'A serving woman took pity on him,' Luc said. 'She took him to her daughter who brought him up as her son.'

'Thank goodness for that. Oh, Luc, what a terrible story.' Jess was shaking her head. 'Your poor family. But surely, what happened that long ago doesn't really—'

'Oh, but it does, Jess.' He took her hand again and stroked it absently. 'You see, I am afraid the Gandillon's are again cursed.'

She began to laugh. 'Oh, Luc . . . you are kidding?'

'Kidding?' His heart plummeted . . . she did not believe him. He had been a fool to think she would.

'Having me on . . . you know . . . telling tales.'

'No, Jess.'

She tossed back her hair. 'Come on, Luc . . . it's a brilliant story but honestly . . . '

He clutched her arms. 'Jess, you must believe me . . . I need your help . . . I need you to . . . '

She stopped laughing and looked into his eyes. Then she wrenched away and stood up.

'I'm going home.'

He grabbed her. 'No, Jess . . . hear me out, please.'

She bit her lip, frowning at him. She must see how desperately he needed her. 'OK,' she sat down again. 'But don't expect me to believe you.'

'Maybe if I take you to see my mother . . . then you will believe me.'

'Your mother? What's she got to do with it?'

'If you listen, I will tell you.'

He saw her expression grow more and more incredulous as he told her. Once, she laughed again then looked angry.

96

Once, she leapt up in terror and tried to run away. He caught her half-way out of the door.

'Please, Jess . . . I need you!'

When he began to cry he heard a small noise of sympathy come from her throat. She put her arms around him, holding him against her while he wept.

'I'm sorry,' she murmured. 'I'm really sorry but it's all so crazy . . . you don't really expect me . . . ?'

He lifted his head and brushed the moisture from his face angrily. 'Please, at least . . . come to see my mother. Then, maybe you will believe me.'

She stared at him in silence for a minute. Then she shrugged. 'OK.'

He took her hand and led her from the kitchen. Past the portraits on the wall, he noticed she averted her gaze. Ah . . . he thought, she almost believes me. I almost have her.

Her hand was tight in his as they stood at the bottom of the curving stairway.

'Do you think she's in her room?' Jess was looking upwards.

'Where else?'

Jess hugged herself. 'Why doesn't she come down by the fire?'

'I do not know. She just prefers to be alone, I think. She has spent almost all her time in her room since my grandparents died.'

'But, Luc, that's years ago. Peggy told me you were only a child.'

'Yes,' he said, his heart turning at the memory. 'I was only a child. But when they died . . . suddenly I had to grow up.'

Jess went up in front of him. Her backside bewitched his eyes. He wanted to put his hand there. Feel the curves. She turned, saw the look on his face. She didn't say anything. He thought she understood.

'Is her room on the next floor?' She stepped on to the first landing. She hugged herself again. 'Luc, it's so cold.

How could someone as sick as your mum live in such a cold place.'

'She does not notice. Next floor up—it is even colder.'

Her footsteps slowed. Near the top, she stopped. She seemed hunched against fear. She had more courage than he thought. Even to have come this far. He could see malevolence whirling down and around her head like a sinister fog. As he watched it seemed to twist and turn . . . forming into some kind of shape.

Luc brushed his hand across his eyes. When he took it away the spectre had gone. His chest heaved in a sigh of relief.

They stepped on to the top landing. Jess stood with her back pressed against the dank wall. There was apprehension in her eyes.

'Luc . . . are you sure it's all right?'

'Yes,' he said. 'It has to be all right.'

The door to his mother's room was closed firmly. He knocked, softly at first, then louder.

'*Maman*? *Maman* . . . may I come in?' He held his breath, straining his ears for her reply. He heard the creak of bedsprings as she rose, then shuffling footsteps across the room.

'What do you want, Luc?' his mother replied eventually.

'I want to come in.'

'Tell her you've brought a friend.' Jess's hands were on his waist.

'No . . . she will not let me in if she knows.'

Luc turned the handle slowly and pushed open the door.

The room was in semi-darkness, the thick curtains drawn, as usual, against the light. The tattered, silken drapes of the huge, mouldering, gold-painted, fourposter bed had been pushed aside. The great, tawny, wolfskin bedcover was thrown back. On the floor, the moth-eaten tapestry carpet was strewn with the remains of leaves and herbs from the forest. Her draped, gilt dressing table was a carnival of old glass perfume bottles and ointment jars. The open doors of the crumbling wardrobes revealed rows of decayed and rotting dresses and coats. Muddied and torn shoes and boots were piled in one corner. His nostrils flared. He despised this room. It symbolized his mother's withdrawal from their world.

She sat in the shadows of the corner opposite the window. Her body, her face, shrouded as always in black. She rocked softly to and fro in her chair. Her boots were still wet and muddy where she had hastened away from Jess in the forest.

She waved a hand. 'What is it, Luc?' Her voice was harsh and pained.

'*Maman* . . . ' Luc reached behind and took Jess's hand. 'I've brought someone to meet you.'

His mother gasped. Her fingers flew upwards. The skin of her hands was reddened and sore, scarred and scratched. Behind him, he heard Jess draw in a sharp breath of shock.

His mother turned her head away, one hand shielding her eyes. The long nails of her other hand plucked nervously the black, muddied cloth of her skirt.

Luc pulled Jess over towards her. '*Maman* . . . ' he whispered. 'It is my friend, Jessica . . . I have wanted to tell you.'

A sharp cry came from his mother's throat. 'Take her away, Luc . . . I beg you.'

'But, *Maman* . . . ?'

Her voice rose into the threat of a scream. 'Luc . . . take her away!'

Behind, Jess was plucking at his jacket. 'Luc, we're upsetting her. Come on, let's go.'

'But, Jess, you *must* see her . . . you'll never believe me unless . . . '

His mother was crying now . . . sobbing . . . 'How can you do this, Luc? Go, please go.'

Jess released the back of his jacket. He heard her run from the room, her boots clattering down the stairs. His lip curled. He went closer and stretched out his hand.

His mother cringed away. 'No, Luc . . . please.'

'It is no good, *Maman*,' he hissed. 'You cannot hide what you are for ever. The girl, Jessica, she is to be your saviour . . . and mine, *Maman*. She is the one.'

He strode over to the window and thrust back the curtains. A shaft of sunlight hit the floor. His mother gave a stifled scream. 'Do not be afraid, *Maman*,' he said. 'You do not have long to wait . . . the night after tomorrow . . . then you will be free.'

Downstairs, Jess was sitting on the settee, her knees drawn up to her chin. She looked up as he came through the door.

'That was one big mistake,' she said.

He spread his hands. 'I know, I am sorry.'

'It's your mum you should apologize to.'

'I have.' He sat beside her. 'You see what she is like.'

'Yes . . . I can see she's really sick. But that doesn't make her . . . a werewolf, for God's sake, Luc. It's just crazy.' She started to rise. 'Look, I've got to go.'

He held her arms and made her look at him. 'Jess, it is not crazy. It is true!' He held her tightly so she could not escape. If she went from him now he knew she would never return. 'Why else does she roam the forest at night? Why else does she come home scratched and bloodied, and tell me this, my Jess, why will she never uncover her face, even in front of her own son?'

Jess shook her head from side to side. She was crying now, tears running down her cheeks. 'I don't know, Luc, I don't know. Maybe she's paranoid . . . maybe she's just scared of the outside world?'

'Of me . . . her son?' he said bitterly. 'Is that why she screams out in agony . . . is that why those animals are always killed on the nights she roams the forest?'

He took a grubby cloth from his pocket and wiped the tears from Jess's face. She had stopped crying and was looking at him with a mixture of horror and realization on her face. His heart leapt in his chest. She believes me, he thought, at last she believes me.

'Is that true,' she whispered. 'When those animals have been killed, your mother is . . . '

'Yes . . . it is true. I have the newspaper cuttings. You must help me, Jess,' he whispered. 'Please.'

She stared into his eyes for a moment. Then she whispered, 'OK, Luc. What do you want me to do?'

He stretched out his finger and lifted the locket from her throat. With his other hand he raised her wrist to his mouth. He laid his lips on the blue vein. He could feel its pulse beneath his touch. Her life's blood. His life's blood. The fingers holding the locket quivered with anticipation.

'A silver phial,' he murmured.

She frowned. 'I don't understand?'

And then he heard it . . . somewhere outside, the sound of men and dogs. He raised his head quickly, suddenly alert.

'Luc . . . what is it?'

He got up swiftly, pushed her away. 'Those people hunting . . . they're almost here.'

'Here?'

His look must have been one of scorn. 'Yes, of course. Where did you think they would come?'

And then he thought he heard another sound. Wild footsteps on the stairs, along the corridor . . . the sound of a window thrust open. *Maman* . . . she had heard them too . . . she was fleeing in panic! Dread clutched at his insides.

'My mother . . . ' he said. 'She has heard them . . . oh God!'

'But, Luc . . . ?' Jess began.

Ignoring her, he lunged across the room and through the door. The sound of the chair he sent spinning echoed behind him. He had forgotten Jess, the locket . . . everything. He had a vision of his mother, running away in panic. Plunging madly through the forest. All he could think about was catching up with her before they did.

He fled down the dusty corridor, past the oil portraits.

101

Their eyes followed, mocked. He thrust open the window and in one huge leap he was through. He landed on all fours. He bounded away across the snowy garden, grass as high as his waist, through the overgrown shrubbery then up over the wall and into the forest.

Behind, Jess's anguished cry faded from his consciousness.

'Luc . . . come back . . . Luc!'

7

JESS

Jess's fist was in her mouth. She watched Luc thrust open the window, dive through and hurtle away across the lawn. The snowy shrubbery closed itself behind him like a clenched fist.

She shouted his name but he didn't come back.

Jess stood there, biting her lip. Where on earth had he gone? Surely you couldn't get out into the forest that way? Then his voice came back to her—*there are secret paths only she knows . . . we have lived in the forest all our lives, remember*? Silence wrapped itself around her. She started suddenly. She heard voices, dogs barking . . . the heavy violent sound of someone knocking on the front door.

Luc had been right. They were coming. Now they were here and somehow she had to convince them they were wasting their time. She glanced upwards at the dark stairs curving away from her. To where, less than half an hour ago Luc's mother had cringed in terror when she saw Jess on the threshold of her room. And now, Luc said, the poor woman had fled in panic from Jack Stride and Peggy like the wild, tormented creature Luc believed she was.

Jess ran her hands through her hair. The whole thing was crazy . . . mad . . . a nightmare.

The knocking came again. Jess ran back along the corridor. She hardly glanced at the portraits but she could feel their eyes following her, watching her every move.

She stood behind the kitchen door, her head pressed against the wall. She closed her eyes.

What shall I do, what shall I tell them? Then Peggy's voice came through the letter box.

'Jess? Luc? Is anyone in there?'

Maybe I should tell them Luc is crazy and his mother desperately ill. Let them find her . . . find Luc . . . take them both away to be looked after. Then she remembered his desperate plea . . . the look of terror and loneliness in his eyes. She couldn't betray him. The world was full of betrayers but she wasn't going to be one of them. He had told her she was the one . . . the one to help him. First—she had to find out exactly what he wanted her to do.

Slowly Jess's hand went to her neck. She could still feel the place where he had nuzzled her. She could still feel his hot breath on her flesh. Her knees felt weak. Her stomach turned over. Why couldn't she just go away, back home to her neat, suburban safety? God, it was like the old nightmare all over again. Danny . . . that bitch, Charlene . . . now this.

The knocking on the front door began again. Jess tore her thoughts from the past. She groped her way back into the present.

'Jess? Luc? You in there?' It was Peggy again.

Jess couldn't stall any longer.

She slowly came to. She brushed the mud off her jeans. She knew she must look terrible. A shiver passed over her. She hated this house. The atmosphere lay heavily around her, suffocating her.

She went out of the back door and looked up into the sky. It had clouded over again. Fresh snow whirled around the portals. Jess drew a deep breath of damp, sharp-edged air. She pulled the edges of her jacket together. Her legs, her feet, the whole of her body was cold now. The icy feeling creeping over her flesh, her bones. She remembered how she had burned with Luc's mouth against her skin.

Round the side of the house the brambles were weighted with snow. Above, the dark windows of the tower were like the vacant eyes of the dead.

Jess glanced up, half expecting to see some wild face looking out. She thought she saw a movement behind the curtain. She knew it must be her imagination. Luc and his mother were both out in the forest somewhere fleeing in terror. Then the wind caught her hair and tossed it over her eyes.

A pair of Alsatians came bounding towards her, barking. She stopped in her tracks, flinched, holding her arms up to protect herself. Jess had never been scared of dogs in her life. Now they seemed a threat.

They skidded to a halt in front of her. Circled her. One came forward to sniff her boots. Jess held herself stiffly as the Alsatian jumped up at her. It put its paws on her shoulders and sniffed her neck. The other one still ran round in circles, sniffing her feet, her legs. A small whine came from its throat.

'Down, Caesar!' Jack Stride came running towards her. He held a shotgun bent in the crook of his arm. His broad face was red with running. Peggy was behind him.

The dog sat obediently at her feet.

'I'm sorry.' Jack clipped the lead on the Alsatian's collar. 'He doesn't usually do that.' He called the other one. 'Cleo! Heel!'

Jess managed a grin. 'It's OK.' She bent to fondle the dog. Her hand was shaking. 'What's all the row about?'

Peggy had followed Jack and was looking at Jess with her usual shrewdness. Jess took a deep breath to calm herself.

'We couldn't make anyone hear,' explained Peggy.

'We were up on the top floor.' Jess looked up. 'Sorry. Anyway, why are you here?' She turned to look at Jack. 'Surely the . . . ' she began innocently.

Jack looked grim. 'The dogs led us here. The creature, puma, panther . . . whatever . . . it must have come this way.'

'Wow!' Jess tried to sound normal. 'Well, Luc never said anything. Maybe it just ran through the grounds or something.'

'Where is the boy?' Jack looked suspicious.

'He's with his mum.' The lie fell easily from her lips. 'She's still really sick.'

'Do you think we could have a word?'

105

Jess stuck out her bottom lip. She shook her head. 'I shouldn't think so actually, not just now. He's staying by her bedside. Honestly, Jack, he'd have said if he'd seen anything.'

Peggy took Jack's arm. 'He would have, Jack. He knows about the beast.'

Jack shrugged. 'OK.' He ran his hand around his jaw. 'Looks like a wild goose chase then.'

Jess saw Peggy glance curiously up at the tower. 'We couldn't get through the gate, it's locked,' she said. 'Doesn't look as if it's ever used.'

'No.' Jess was surprised how calm she sounded. 'You have to climb the wall.'

'Yes.' Peggy looked down at her filthy jeans. 'So we found out. The dogs went straight over so we had to follow.'

They strolled round to the front of the house pushing aside the brambles, the snow-laden shrubbery, as they went. There were two other men waiting by the front door. One in the dark uniform of the RSPCA. The other wore a green waxed jacket, trousers tucked in black wellington boots. He held an evil looking Dobermann on a short lead.

'Nothing here by the looks of it,' Jack called.

'We'll just take a look round the other side.' The other two went off with the Dobermann.

'Take Cleo,' Jack called. One of the men whistled and the Alsatian bounded off, disappeared round the corner.

'There's nothing round there,' Jess called but they ignored her.

'Shall we go back?' Peggy held Jack's arm. Jess felt surprised. It wasn't like Peggy to look to someone else for a decision. It was strange what love could do. It could turn you into someone else . . . someone stupid . . . blind . . .

Jack took off his cap and scratched his head. He shrugged. 'I suppose we'd better.' He bit his lip, frowning. 'It's odd, it's really odd.' He bent to stroke Caesar. 'Something definitely came through here. There was no stopping the dogs.' He looked up at the overhanging eaves of the house. He shook his head. 'Odd . . . very odd.'

'I'll walk back with you if you like, Peggy,' Jess said. The sooner they got away from here, the better.

Peggy smiled at her. 'Come on, then. No point in freezing to death.'

Suddenly there was a shout. 'Round here . . . we've found something.'

No!

The Dobermann had its paws on the windowsill. Its dark nose sniffed, claws scratched. It leapt up, trying to get inside the open window. The lead held it back.

'I'll let him off.'

'No!' Jess plunged forward. 'Luc's mother will be scared if he gets inside. Please . . . there's nothing here. He can probably smell a cat or something.'

She felt Peggy give her an odd look.

'Cleo's off!' The man in the waxed jacket plunged forward, following the Alsatian bitch as she headed for the shrubbery. The other man released the Dobermann. Caesar bounded off after it. The three dogs barked. They disappeared and Jess could hear them charging about in circles trying to pick up the scent.

'Come on,' Jack said hurriedly, 'or we'll lose the blasted dogs as well.'

Peggy hung back. 'Jess?'

'You go. I'm off home.'

Peggy hesitated. 'Go on,' Jess said. 'You'll lose them.'

Jess ran back along the forest path. There seemed suddenly an atmosphere of grey evil in the place she had always thought so friendly. In the distance, the startled hammer-noise of a pheasant broke the heavy silence. Once or twice she glanced over her shoulder at sounds behind her. The plop . . . plop . . . as damp wodges of snow fell from the branches. The shock of Luc's story crashed in on her. His

107

mother... a werewolf... the whole thing was potty. *I should belt home as fast as I can... pack my bags... scarper.* But she couldn't spend the rest of her life running away. She had to help Luc, she had to. Even if he was crazy, it didn't mean he did not need help.

Out of breath, Jess slowed down at the fork in the path. There was a swish behind her, a crack as a twig broke. She turned swiftly. There was nothing there. Only a soft thud as a parcel of snow fell from a branch. She jogged on, following the deep footprints she had made on her way in. Once, she slipped and clutched at an overhanging branch for support. It was then that she heard it again . . . a sound like the soft padding of footfalls in the trees behind her. A broad wave of fear enveloped her. She glanced round, then began to run as swiftly as she could. Ahead she could see the edge of the forest, the pathway she had woven through the snow leading up the slope to safety. Her breath came out in jagged gasps. Her chest ached. *This is stupid, crazy... there's nothing there . . . nothing.*

She hurtled out from the forest edge, turning to glance over her shoulder as she ran. Behind, a long-legged tawny shadow dissolved into the mist and was gone.

Jess struggled up the hill, gasping for breath. She clambered over the gate and headed for the house. Gradually her painful gasps subsided. She turned and looked down into the forest. Then she began to giggle.

'God,' she said aloud, 'I'm going nuts.'

'Jess . . . ' The sound of her name came from behind the feedstore.

She jumped, then turned quickly. 'Luc . . . ' she held her hand to her chest. 'God, you made me jump again. Thank goodness you're here. They picked up your tracks and went off after you like bats out of hell.'

'Yes,' he said, 'I know.'

He came to her. He was wet, filthy. His hair matted with thorns and twigs. His jeans were torn, one arm of his leather jacket almost ripped off. There was blood on his face.

She put out her hand to touch him. 'Luc! What on earth's happened to you?'

'Please,' he took her arm, looking round like a frightened animal, 'may we go indoors?'

'Yes, of course.' Jess fumbled in her inside pocket for the key. 'On the way back—' Jess began.

'What . . . ?'

'Nothing . . . I thought someone . . . something was following me. It wasn't you, was it?'

Luc shook his head. 'No, it was not me.'

Indoors, the fire was low. Jess wrenched off her coat, wet from dripping snow. She wondered where the others were. Peggy and Jack . . . the other two . . . the dogs. Were they still somewhere deep in the forest, chasing illusions?

Jess opened the stove door, threw on a log.

She made Luc sit down by the hearth. The cat had already gone from the chair, leaped off with a scared yowl as Luc came through the door.

Outside, the kennel dogs had set up their baleful howling.

Jess was busy boiling the kettle. She found a bowl, some disinfectant.

She saw Luc sway towards the warmth, his head in his hands.

She brought the things to him, knelt in front.

'Take off your jacket.'

She unzipped it for him then helped him shrug it off his shoulders.

He was naked underneath. His shoulder bled where his jacket had been torn away.

'How did this happen?'

'I fell,' he said simply.

'You didn't catch up with your mother?'

He shook his head. 'No . . . I could not find her.'

Jess bathed the place gently. He didn't flinch when she applied diluted disinfectant to a deep cut on his shoulder. 'I wish I understood all this, Luc . . . OK, you've told me

109

about your ancestors, and the curse, but I still don't understand what you want me to do.'

'I will tell you now.'

'Good,' she said. She reached up and bathed his cheek then dried it softly with a towel. She saw he was watching her face. She knew he really needed her so how could she refuse to help him, to do what he asked? When he leaned to kiss her there was fire snaking through her veins.

When he drew away she whispered, 'I never thought I'd care about anyone again . . . not the way I cared about Danny.' Her voice sounded strange, crackly. She ran her fingertips over the sleek, hard muscles of his chest.

'Do you care about me that way?' he asked softly.

How could she help it? He was so beautiful. Like a haunted wild creature. She swallowed.

'Come off it. Would I help you otherwise?' She tried to joke.

He put his hand on her shoulder. 'You will help me, then?'

She rose and took the bowl to the sink. She stood with her hands on the edge of the draining board. Her knees were shaking. Then she turned. 'Luc . . . I still don't know if I believe what you've told me or not. I must be mad, but I will help you. What do you want me to do?'

She came to kneel in front of him. She laid her head in his lap against the hard ridges of his abdominal muscles. She heard his breath quicken.

'Poor Luc . . . ' She reached up to touch his face. Her fingers traced the line of his jaw.

He caught her thin wrist, turned it to kiss the place where the blood pulsed.

'Jess . . . ' she could feel his breath on her skin. 'We've got to get this thing finished.' She saw him glance out of the window where the snow-laden day seemed almost night. 'Before it's too late.'

'Yes . . . but how?'

Jess watched him as he leaned down and picked his jacket

off the floor. He drew a small, ancient, leather-bound book from the inside pocket.

'This book,' he said. 'I found it in the library at Spital House.' He opened the flyleaf and turned it round so Jess could see. *Folklore and Charms Against Werewolves* it was called.

'I have read it so many times,' he said, 'I know parts of it by heart. The parts that tell tales of men and women who turn into wolves, hunting and killing at night. It describes the way they looked . . . scarred hands and feet, red teeth, and growths of hair on their faces and bodies . . . look.' He opened another page for Jess to see. There was an eighteenth-century engraving of a clawed monster with a wolf's head devouring a maiden. Before she could comment, Luc turned the page again, flicking through until he found the part he wanted. He handed her the book. 'Read it, Jess.'

Jess read aloud.

'*A Charm Against Werewolves.*

'*When the moon is full and ripe, three drops of blood in a silver phial from a rich and willing maiden shall be rubbed on the nose of the cursed one. Then all the pleasant folk will sing the song of the forests and their dwelling places will become safe havens of peace.*'

He was looking at her, his eyes were pleading, like a child.

'That is you, Jess,' he said, taking the book from her hand. 'Jessica . . . the wealthy one. And you are a maiden . . . you told me you had not . . . had not made love with Danny . . . You see, Jess, it has to be you.' He lowered his eyes and fiddled with the back of his hand. Then he looked at her again. 'Jess. I am so scared . . . scared that the curse is on me, too. That one day I shall become like her.'

Jess drew in her breath. 'But, Luc . . . ?' she began.

He took hold of her arms. 'Jess . . . please. All I need is six drops of your blood, three for her and three for me.'

Jess heaved a sigh. Was it too much to ask? Six drops of

her blood? Six drops to get rid of the terrors that haunted him.

'OK, Luc,' she said at last. 'If that's what you want.'

She saw relief flood his eyes. His grip tightened on her arms. 'Thank you, Jess.' He rose. 'I had better go. They will be back soon. They should not find me here.'

Jess stood up too. 'Peggy won't mind.'

He shook his head. 'No . . . I do not want to see her. Perhaps when this is all over, I shall not be so afraid.'

She put a hand on his arm. 'Luc, when . . . when do you want me to do this . . . this thing?'

'The night after tomorrow,' he said. 'When the moon is full.'

She dropped her gaze. He was so certain . . . so certain that some magic charm he'd found in an old book was the answer to his prayers. Well . . . who was she to argue?

Luc picked up his jacket.

'Hey, you can't wear that. Here . . . ' she went to the row of coats by the back door and unhooked a red, checked lumberjack's coat. 'Borrow this. Peggy won't mind. I'll ask her if she'll mend yours, she's good at sewing and stuff.'

'Thank you.'

Jess suddenly felt afraid. How was she to do . . . this thing he was asking, if his mother wouldn't let her near? When she was asleep perhaps . . . what if she woke up and . . . ?

'Luc,' she began, 'I don't know if I'm brave enough.'

He took her hands between his own. 'Jess, you are my only hope.' He touched her hair, rubbed a tendril between his fingertips. 'And you are brave, I have seen how brave you can be.'

She held up the coat. 'Can you put your arm through?'

She held one side out for him. He winced with pain, easing his arm inside the sleeve.

He took her face between his hands. 'You will come tomorrow, Jess?' he whispered.

'Yes, I will, I promise.'

'When?'

112

'I'm not sure . . . as soon as I can, OK?'

'Very well. You will need to stay until it is dark.'

'Yes,' she said. 'I know.'

Outside, it had stopped snowing. The darkening sky was still leaden with a promise of more. The ponies were standing, fetlock high, a little way along by the fence. They tossed their heads, snorted as Luc climbed over the gate.

'They're waiting to be fed.' Jess leaned her arms on the top rail. Her breath came out in a spiral of grey. 'Greedy pigs. It's all they think about, food.'

Luc put his hands in his pockets, hunched his shoulders against the cold.

'Luc,' said Jess. 'I don't understand . . . why haven't you got help before? All those years with your mother when she's been so ill?'

'She would not let me. Even when I ran to the village when my grandparents died, she would not see anyone. That was before I realized what she was. When I found out . . . I understood why.' Jess looked at him for a minute and she knew he could still see doubt in her eyes. 'You must trust me, Jess,' he pleaded. 'You are the only one.'

'Am I really the one . . . the only one?'

He nodded. 'Yes. I have waited for you all my life.'

Her nose was red with cold. Moisture seeped from her eyes. She swallowed and wrapped her arms around herself for comfort. She combed her hair back with her fingers. 'That's what he said,' she muttered.

'Who?'

'Danny.'

Luc put his hand on her shoulder. 'You must forget Danny. He is dead, gone. It is me . . . Luc . . . I am here now. I need you now, Jess.'

'I know.' When she looked at him, she didn't know if the pity in his eyes was for her, or for himself. '*He* said he needed me,' she said bitterly. 'That I was the only one.'

113

'But you were not?'

She shook her head wordlessly.

'When did you find out?'

'After he died. There was this girl . . . Charlene . . . '
Voice breaking, she told him the rest.

It seemed crazy, standing out here in the freezing cold,
telling Luc the bit she had been unable to tell him before.

'Your friend, Emma?' he said. 'Why did she not tell you
sooner?'

'She said she didn't want to hurt me.'

'It would have been better if she had.'

Jess looked away, down the hill. 'Yes—although I should
have guessed. If I hadn't been so stupid and blind.'

Luc touched her shoulder in sympathy.

'When I look back,' Jess went on, still hugging herself
against the cold wind. 'It was pretty obvious. All that stuff
about loving me . . . he was having me on . . . playing a
game.'

Luc leaned towards her, put an arm round her neck and
drew her to him. Between them, the frozen steel of the gate
was like a metal stake against their hearts.

'I am sorry,' he murmured. 'I am so sorry.'

She raised her head defiantly. 'Don't be, Luc. He was a
bastard. A real bastard. I was just too stupid to see it. He
was really good-looking and he had this motor bike . . . '
She shrugged impatiently. 'He was the first bloke I really
went out with . . . fell . . . '

' . . . fell in love with?' Luc finished her sentence.

Jess nodded. 'Everyone else fancied him too . . . he used
to roar up on his bike to meet me from college. I used to
feel proud, really special, you know?' She shook her head.
'I must have been nuts.'

Luc touched her cheek. 'No . . . just vulnerable. It is not a
crime.'

She took a handkerchief from her pocket and blew her
nose. She smiled quickly. 'No.'

Jess stiffened suddenly. 'I can hear the Land Rover,' she

said. 'If you don't want them to see you, you'd better go.'

Luc turned to run. 'You will come tomorrow?' he called.

'Yes.'

She watched him as he ran down the hill. He turned once to wave then disappeared into the forest.

'Tomorrow . . . ' Jess thought with a shiver of anticipation. 'The night after tomorrow.'

As she turned to go back indoors, Jack's Land Rover pulled into the yard. Peggy got out. Jack waved to Jess then turned the vehicle and drove off back down the drive.

'How did you get on?' Jess asked.

Peggy pulled a face. 'No luck, the dogs lost the scent—we didn't even get out of the garden.'

'What are you going to do?'

'Wait until next time I suppose . . . that's if there is a next time. Let's hope there isn't. Come on indoors. Some of that soup will go down a treat.'

Indoors, Peggy stood in front of the fire rubbing her hands together. 'Hey,' she said suddenly. 'Is that Luc's coat?'

'Oh . . . yes.' Jess picked it up. 'It got torn. I said maybe you'd mend it. You're good at that kind of thing.'

'Was he here, then?' Peggy's eyebrows knitted together.

'Yes. You don't mind do you?'

'No, of course not, dear girl. But I thought he was at home with his mother?'

Jess thought quickly. She hated telling fibs to Peggy but she couldn't betray him.

'He was . . . he sneaked out and followed me back here.'

Peggy frowned. 'He's really odd, that boy.'

'Yes.'

'Actually,' Peggy went on, 'you left the back door open . . . we went into the kitchen. Honestly, Jess, I'm a lousy housekeeper but what a mess!'

'Yes,' Jess said. 'I know.'

'Luc's mother must have heard us . . . when we left, she was looking out from the curtains in one of those rooms in

115

the tower. That's a bloody creepy place. I don't know how anyone can live there. You know I've half a mind to have a word with the doctor. I don't care if they think I'm nosy or not.'

'But . . . ?' Jess began.

Peggy waved her hand. 'Oh, I know I'm always on about freedom of choice and all that . . . but she needs medical help, Jess. She's *entitled* to it, isn't she?'

Jess frowned. How on earth could Luc's mother be in the tower room if she had run off into the forest.

'Are you sure it was her?' she asked.

'Yes . . . it certainly wasn't Luc, we could see that much. He was obviously on his way here by then, anyway.'

'Yes,' said Jess, still frowning. 'I suppose he must have been.'

8

LUC

The wind stung his face as he turned and ran off down the hill. He twisted his head. He needed one last look at her. She was standing by the fence watching him go. He waved once. Then he saw the vehicle's headlights wash over the brow of the hill and swing into the yard. He turned and disappeared into the forest.

At the place where the path forked in two, Luc swung off left and headed for the caves. He wanted to see if his mother was there. Earlier, he realized he had lost her tracks as soon as he fled from the house after her. He had been terrified at first, terrified the dogs would track her down. Now . . . when he thought about it, he almost laughed out loud. She had escaped them as she had escaped before, eluding even him, her son, who knew the forest almost as well as she. Fools if they thought they could ever hunt her down. And soon . . . tomorrow, there would be no forest beast to pursue and no one but Jess would ever know the secret of the family Gandillon.

Jess . . . his heart lurched at the thought of her. She had wanted him earlier, he had been able to tell. It had been all he could do to control his excitement. She was fascinated by him. His eyes, his skin. She had hardly been able to keep her hands from him. And what would he do when it was all over. When she had gone back home to her suburban safety? Luc was beginning to think he could never let her go. When he first saw her, walking in the forest, he had a wild vision. He would capture her and keep her with him always. Like that prince in the fairytale . . . the one who had been turned into a beast. He had been dreaming, of course, letting his fantasies intrude on reality . . . it was the story of

117

his life. And now . . . how could he ever let her go? He had planned it all so carefully. She was to be his saviour but he had never dreamed he would really love her.

He reached the cave, slipping and sliding on the boulders strewn in front of the entrance. He was panting, sweating . . . the wool of the borrowed coat harsh against his naked skin.

He stood at the entrance, head tilted to one side, listening.

'*Maman?*' he called softly. '*Maman* . . . there is no one here but me . . . it is safe to come out.'

He peered into the gloom. The cave was high and deep . . . a perfect place to hide. He had been in there several times. There were old, discarded bones, shreds of cloth, dried bracken piled into a nest, the smell of an animal. He knew it was where she came to hide away from him.

'*Maman?*' he called again. Louder this time. He strained his ears for sounds from within. It seemed he could hear something. A low, threatening growl from deep in the cave. Then, from out of the gloom, a dark shape seemed to be slinking towards him. He thought he heard the growl again . . . a low rumble like a rumour of distant thunder. Then a whine. The shadow slid to a halt. Luc narrowed his eyes . . . twin points of fire seemed to be pinning him to the spot.

Luc snorted derisively. 'I am not frightened of you, *Maman*,' he whispered.

He waited but the shadow remained still, crouched, low, indistinguishable from the darkness itself.

'Very well, *Maman*,' he said at last. 'I am going back now.'

He turned and jogged back the way he had come. He was stupid to think she would come out even though daylight had almost gone. He shrugged. She would crawl home later when he was sleeping. He knew her habits of old. Sneaking back home before first light. Did she think he was deaf that he did not hear her soft footfalls on the stair? Stupid to think she had merely been out gathering her wild plants.

Well, Maman, *soon you will not need to go out at night* . . .

118

to hide your beautiful face from me, your own son. He felt tears spring to his eyes. *Soon,* Maman, *you will be able to read those stories to me . . . as you did when I was a child . . . soon,* Maman . . . *soon.*

At home, he burst into the kitchen. He wrenched off the rough jacket and lit the lamp. On the table, in a brown dish, were the remains of the meal his mother had prepared earlier. So she had been back to eat? He felt relieved. At least if her stomach was full then the animals at the sanctuary would be safe tonight.

He scraped the mess into a saucepan and put it on the stove, stirring it round and round with a grimy wooden spoon that had lain in the sink. His mouth watered as he suddenly realized he had not eaten all day.

When the food had heated through, he sat on the settee, spooning it into his mouth straight from the saucepan. At last, full up, he slung the dirty pan in the sink and lay back. He felt good, sleepy. He pushed his hair back from his face. His arm was stiff but would soon heal. His chest heaved in a deep sigh. He wished Jess were there to share his contentment. For the first time for as long as he could remember, he looked forward to tomorrow. He dozed fitfully, rising once to throw a log on the fire. Above, shadows danced on the ceiling. Suddenly he noticed a grey mist hovering near the window. His heart began to hammer unevenly in his chest. Fear became a lead weight in his throat. His palms started to sweat. The mist whirled and spiralled. It began to shift into shape . . . an ashen face . . . arms . . .

No . . . !

Luc leapt up and plunged from the room. He slammed the door shut then stood with his back to it for a moment, panting with fear. Then he bolted down the corridor and up the stairs to the first landing. He stopped, peering back the way he had come. A slender shaft of light from the waxing moon speared the staircase below him. He drew a sobbing breath. Then he ran on up to the second landing. Outside his mother's door he flung himself to the floor, sitting with his knees drawn up to his chin. When she returns, he thought, trying to calm himself, she will find me here, waiting.

He sat with his back against her door, wishing the long night away. He laid his forehead on his knees. He must have dozed off for when an owl screeched from the trees he opened his eyes with a start. For a moment he was confused, not knowing where he was or what he was doing there. Moonlight made shadows reality. He hunched his shoulders and clenched his fingers together. He stared at the backs of his hands. The hairs seemed to be growing longer as he watched. He groaned, convinced his worst fears were coming true. He tried to calm himself, drawing deep, shuddering breaths.

Eventually, when his terror subsided, he curled up on the cold floor and swapped the ghost of his panic for a tossing, restless sleep.

9

JESS

Next morning, Jess woke early. She felt scared but full of determination. Her chores took no time at all. She even hummed as she worked. She came back indoors, stoked the fire, then cooked herself breakfast. Egg, toast, baked beans. She made some for Peggy and took it up to her.

'Breakfast, madam,' Jess sounded more cheerful than she felt.

Peggy opened her eyes and sat up quickly. 'Christ, Jess what's the time?' She glanced at the clock. It was gone nine o'clock. Outside, the early mist had cleared, the ghostly hint of a full moon just visible in a sky that promised to be blue. Peggy pushed her hair from her face. 'I haven't slept this late in years.'

'Do you good,' Jess said. She set the tray down on Peggy's lap. 'I came to tell you I'm off to see Luc. He wants me to do something for him. I've fed the ponies and let the dogs out into their runs.'

'This is great,' Peggy said with a grin. 'Don't fancy staying here permanently do you?'

'As a matter of fact I'd love to,' Jess said with a smile.

'Jess,' Peggy said more seriously, 'I've been thinking . . . I don't know if you should go to Luc's again.'

'You sound like my mum.'

'I'm sorry, I'm not trying to tell you what to do but . . . '

Jess sat on the bed. 'I've got to, Peggy, I promised, I can't let him down.'

'What is it he wants you to do?'

Jess lowered her eyes. She twisted her hands together in her lap. 'I can't tell you, I'm sorry.'

'Are you sure you know what you're doing, Jess?' Peggy

leaned forward. 'OK, I know I sound like your mother but I did promise her I'd look after you.'

'I can look after myself, Peggy.'

'I know, darling. I'm sorry. Look, I've got to go into the village this morning. I'm going to have a word with Doctor Prentiss, I honestly think she should try and see Luc's mother.'

'Yes, so do I. She's really sick. I saw her yesterday too . . . well . . . ' Jess hesitated.

'You saw her? Why didn't you tell me?' Peggy said with a mouthful of toast.

'I don't know.'

Peggy pushed the tray aside. 'Well . . . go on . . . how was she . . . what did she look like? We couldn't see her face properly yesterday, she had some kind of scarf on.'

Jess rose and went to the window. The snow was already beginning to melt, dripping steadily from rooftops and branches. She drew a deep breath, then turned to face her aunt.

'Peggy . . . I think she's a bit mad . . . I think Luc is too.'

Peggy's face was grim. 'Go on.'

Jess bit her lip. 'He's got some crazy idea in his head that the family are . . . ' It was no good, Jess couldn't bring herself to say it.

Peggy pushed back the quilt and swung her legs over the side of the bed. She dressed quickly, pulling on a thick sweater and jeans, two pairs of woolly socks. ' . . . are what, Jess?'

'Are cursed in some kind of way.' She had thought Peggy would laugh but she didn't. She stood in front of the mirror running a comb through her long hair. She bunched it together at the back of her head and fixed it with an elastic band. She frowned at Jess in the mirror. 'What, you mean they're paranoid?'

'Yes . . . kind of. He reads all those old books, about folklore and stuff, it's given him really strange ideas . . . '

'What about you . . . what do you think about his mum?'

'I don't know,' Jess said again. 'I know she's very ill, and needs help . . . and I guess he does too.'

Peggy put down the comb. 'Well, that's really made up my mind. Look, Jess, you be careful?'

'Yes, I will. You know, I'm the only friend Luc has ever had. I feel guilty even telling you this much, as if I've betrayed him.'

'Did you promise him you wouldn't tell anyone?'

'No.'

Peggy gave her a hug. 'Well, then. I'll see what I can do.'

'They won't want anyone just barging in.'

'I know. I'll discuss it with the doctor . . . we'll think of something, don't worry.'

Jess picked up Peggy's tray. 'Peggy . . . I probably won't be back until after dark . . . you're not to worry about me, OK?'

Peggy looked uncertain. 'Yes, all right. If you want to ring me, I'll come round by road and pick you up.'

Jess shook her head. 'No, they don't have a phone. Luc will walk back with me, he can find his way in the dark.'

'Well . . . be careful. That animal's hiding up somewhere in the forest, it could well be about. Has Luc got a gun?'

'I don't know, but we'll be OK, honestly.'

Peggy bit her lip. She looked as if she was about to say something else but changed her mind.

Jess was wearing her leather jacket and boots. She always felt different, wearing those things. Brave and somehow defiant . . . invincible, like a warrior. The shiny studs, the zips . . . she remembered her mother's acid comments when she first came home with the jacket.

'Your father says you look like one of those bikers,' she had said.

Jess had never known why her father couldn't tell her that himself.

But Danny had said she looked great . . . as if she'd been

born to wear leather. It seemed odd, thinking about Danny without pain. As if doing so had already become a habit.

Walking through the forest towards Luc's house Jess suddenly realized something.

I'm over it . . . I'm really over Danny!

It was as if a great burden had been lifted from her shoulders. And she knew she had Luc to thank for that. She owed him. She began to skip along, slipping and sliding on the slushy path.

'I'm over it,' she shouted out loud, smiling to herself like an idiot. 'I'm really over it.'

Then, as she sobered up, the weight of Luc's request came crashing in on her.

Six drops of virgin's blood in a silver phial. Three for my mother and three for me.

She unzipped the top of her jacket. Her fingers sought and found the silver locket at her throat. She felt a pang of apprehension. Then she shrugged. It was a really crazy thing to ask someone to do. But it couldn't do any harm . . . a small cut on her finger, six drops squeezed out . . . it would be no worse than having a blood test. And if it made Luc feel better . . . if he was convinced her blood would drive the demons from his mother . . . then what did it matter? That was if she could get near enough to his mother to do it.

Suddenly, her courage waned. Apprehension clenched her insides. She slowed the rush of her eager footsteps. She tried to remember what she knew about werewolves. The movies she had seen. All she could remember was laughing at some man growing hair . . . his hands . . . his face . . . then looking at himself in the mirror. She had never been keen on those horror movies most of her friends adored. All she could think of was that everyone in the cinema had cracked up. Werewolves, she had thought . . . and pigs might fly!

Suddenly Luc was there beside her.

At the side of the path, the bushes that had silently disgorged him gave a slight shiver. Her hand flew to her chest. She gave a small, nervous laugh. 'Luc, don't keep doing this to me!'

'I am sorry.' He slid his arm around her shoulders as if she belonged to him. He had tied his hair back in its long, soft pony-tail. His eyes looked bright gold in the morning's snow-light. There was a shadow of dark-golden hair on his jaw. He still wore Peggy's lumberjack's coat. 'I knew you were coming,' he murmured softly. 'I ran to meet you. You came sooner than I had thought.'

'Yes,' she said. 'I thought, once I got here, there would be no turning back.'

'There is no need to be afraid, Jess.'

She looked up at him. 'Luc, she's never going to let me do it, you know that, don't you?'

'She will be asleep. I promise you.'

Jess remembered him telling her about the infusion of herbs he made to help his mother rest.

'OK . . . Luc, I still think you've got hold of the wrong end of the stick.'

'Stick?' he frowned.

'I mean I think you've got it all wrong.'

'No, Jess,' he insisted. 'I have not got it wrong. Once you have done as I have asked, you will see . . . everything will be all right. My mother will be cured.'

Jess sighed. 'I hope you're right.' She took his hand into her own. 'Luc, I want something in return for this. You're not getting off that lightly, you know.'

He looked at her, his eyes glowing with light. 'Anything.'

'I want you to promise me you'll allow a doctor to see your mum.'

A slight frown crossed his brow. 'But do you not see, my Jess, she will not need a doctor . . . she will be cured.'

'Luc . . . ?'

But nothing she could say after that would convince him he was wrong. She felt his arm hug her tightly and saw a flush come to his cheeks. He stopped walking and spun her to face him.

'Jess, you must believe me!'

She touched his cheek. 'Honestly, Luc,' she murmured, 'I don't know what I believe. All I know is that I want to help you.'

She saw his chest heave in a great sigh. He bent to kiss her, lifting her to him. With his mouth on hers he seemed to breathe into her all the years of his terror and frustration, of anger and dread. She closed her eyes. Suddenly she knew what it was like to live like that . . . always to be afraid. It was as if he had let her into his heart.

'You are the one,' she heard him murmur against her mouth. 'My lovely Jess, you are the one.' And as he drew away she heard him whisper, 'Now all we have to do is wait.' Then he let her go and ran ahead, jumping high in the air. He clenched his hand into a fist and punched the sky. 'One more day's light . . . ' he shouted joyfully. 'One more day's light!'

Near the house, Jess halted. 'Luc . . . I'm really scared.'

He still had his arm round her, supporting her. 'Jess?'

She swallowed nervously. 'Sorry, I'm OK, really. I just don't want to go in . . . not yet.'

'You will get cold out here.'

'Isn't there somewhere else we can go . . . to the village, perhaps. We could go to the pub . . . '

He shook his head vehemently. 'No . . . I cannot.'

Jess looked at her watch. It was about five hours to dusk. Where could they go?

'There is an outbuilding,' he said suddenly. 'I sleep there sometimes. It is not very nice, but I can make a fire . . . '

'OK,' she said.

They climbed the wall.

'This way.' Luc took her hand and guided her across what had once been a beautiful lawn. He took her through a doorway in the kitchen garden wall. Across the other side there was a brick building, a half shattered door was open.

126

Inside it was grey and damp. A moist, acid smell of something rotting assaulted her nostrils. A pile of mouldering blankets were curled in a corner. There was a small rusted woodstove.

Jess looked around. She shuddered. 'It's more creepy than the house.'

He shrugged. 'I am sorry.'

They found wood and lit the fire. The floor was encrusted with bird droppings, bits of straw and leaves. Jess cleared a space with the toe of her boot. She sat, legs crossed, holding out her hands to the warmth.

She suddenly remembered a Mars bar in her pocket. She'd bought it when she went to the shop that first day . . . *Cattle slaughtered in frenzied attack.* The headlines crashed into her memory.

She pushed the vision aside, took out the chocolate bar and pulled it in half.

'No, thank you,' Luc shook his head.

'Aren't you hungry?'

'No. Jess . . . ' He took her hand and toyed with her fingers. She saw him feel the bones with his fingertips. He would not look at her. 'Jess,' he said again. 'When this is over, I want . . . '

She waited for him to go on.

'I want you to stay here with me . . . I . . . cannot let you go, Jess.'

Jess felt her eyes fill with tears. 'Luc, I'd really like to but I can't . . . I have to go back to college. I'll come to visit whenever I can but I can't stay here for ever.'

He dropped his gaze, his mouth turning down in disappointment.

She put her hand on his leg, feeling the hard muscles of his thighs beneath her fingertips. 'Luc, you must do something with your life. You can't spend it hidden away here in the forest . . . there's so much to see and do.'

He snorted air through his nostrils. 'And where do you think I would fit in, Jess?'

127

'You don't have to *fit in* anywhere, Luc. You can do what you like . . . go where you like.'

He shrugged and she saw fear in his eyes. 'I do not know.'

'Maybe you could come and stay with me?'

He laughed then. 'I do not think I would be very welcome in your mother's neat house.'

Jess shook her head. 'I'm not having all that again. It was bad enough with Danny. I'll leave home . . . find a flat or something.' She grinned. 'You could come and live with me, Luc . . . hey, that would be great.'

He smiled suddenly. 'Yes . . . that would be great.'

He put his arm around her and gave her a quick, wild kiss. 'When my mother is better, I will do that. The family Gandillon will no longer be cursed. I will be free, my Jessica . . . I will be free.' He put his hands into her hair. His eyes washed over her face. 'Jess . . . when you go to my mother, I do not want you to be afraid.'

'No,' said Jess, sounding braver than she felt. 'I won't.'

Jess didn't know how long it was that they sat there. Luc got up now and then to feed the flames then came back, pulling her close. When they warmed up, he took off the harsh wool jacket. Again, he was naked underneath.

'Have you lost all your sweatshirts?' She put her arm round, under his, then joined her hands the other side. She could feel his ribs, the hard muscles of his back.

He shrugged. 'I forgot to put one on. My mind was on other things.'

'Don't you feel the cold?' she murmured.

'Sometimes.'

'Do you work out?' She let go her other hand and ran her fingers over his chest. She felt his nipples go hard.

'Work out?' He looked down at her, puzzled. His eyes were hooded, gilded with mist.

'Umm, lift weights . . . you know.' Her voice was dreamy, far away.

He smiled. 'No.'

She felt him stir beneath her fingers. 'Jess . . . ' he shifted his position beside her.

'Umm . . . ?' It was crazy but she felt so relaxed, at peace. The warmth of the fire was even making her sleepy. Perhaps he had cast a spell on her . . . a charm . . . a charm against werewolves.

He hesitated. 'There . . . there's something else I have to tell you.'

She sat up, stared at him. 'What?'

'If she bites you . . . you will become like her. I read it. People who are bitten by werewolves become cursed themselves.' He lowered his glance, then put his head in her lap. 'I am sorry,' his voice was muffled against her thighs. 'I should have told you before.'

Jess swallowed. This was crazy. Was he really telling her that if his mother should wake, she would try to bite her?

'It's a great time to tell me!' She made her voice light. She couldn't chicken out now, not once she'd made up her mind.

He looked up. 'I . . . was not going to tell you but . . . '

'But what?'

'I . . . I decided I had to.'

'Why?'

He raised his head to look at her. 'Because I love you. Because I have to give you one last chance to change your mind.'

She sighed. 'I can't, Luc. I can't let you down. It'll be OK. I'll be gentle as a lamb . . . she won't wake up, I promise.'

Luc didn't answer.

'And what about you?' she said. 'Will you bite me when I do it to you?'

'No,' he said. 'I shall love you.'

The heat of the fire was dying down. Luc rose to throw on another log. He paced over to the window and gazed out at

129

the darkening sky. Then he turned and came back to her. He put out his hands and gently unzipped her jacket. He lifted up the silver chain at her throat.

'The silver phial,' he whispered. His fingers trembled. 'It is almost time, Jess,' he whispered.

Jess reached back and undid the clasp. She let the locket fall into his outstretched hand. She unsnapped the locket. It lay, an open heart on her palm.

Luc took a knife from his belt and slid it from its sheath. The white steel blade glinted in the firelight.

Strangely, Jess felt no fear. She held out her index finger. 'Here,' she said.

Without hesitation Luc quickly flashed the blade across her skin. She drew in her breath, swallowed the deep, sharp shock of pain. The blood oozed . . . first a single drop . . . then another . . . another . . .

Luc took her finger and squeezed it over the open locket. When the tiny vessel was full he put her finger into his mouth. She felt his lips close around the wound.

'Luc!' She wanted to pull away but somehow she couldn't.

'I am sorry,' he let her go. He snapped the locket shut. 'Keep it safe, Jess,' he whispered. 'You have my life in your hand.'

They sat in silence then, until the cold blue faded into twilight and the full moon rose like a great silver coin in the sky.

1 0

LUC

Luc sat, his arms folded around her. Her head was on his shoulder and he thought she was asleep. In her hand, she clutched the locket.

He stared into space. He frowned and narrowed his eyes. A mist seemed to be creeping in through the window, swirling towards him like a grey spiral of chiffon. Luc flared his nostrils. There was a smell . . . he knew what it was. The smell of roots and herbs that grew wild in the forest. He had smelt it a hundred times before. Hellebore, monkshood, nightshade . . . he knew them from the wild bouquets his mother combed from the forest. The movement came again. His hands began to sweat with fear. His throat felt dry. He rubbed his eyes. The spectre that had haunted him for as long as he could remember seemed at last to be weaving itself into some kind of shape. It had come now to plague him in the last hour before the rest of his life.

'Not now,' Luc hissed in terror. 'Please . . . not now.'

It looked like a figure . . . a man . . . mixing something up in a wooden bowl. The hazy image had hovered on the edge of his vision since he was a boy. And now, at last, Luc could see it quite clearly. The man wore rough clothes, strange yet oddly familiar. A grubby shirt made of some kind of coarse linen, a pale waistcoat . . . a neckerchief . . . brown knee breeches. He seemed to be mumbling something . . . a spell . . . an incantation. As Luc watched, the ghost-man took the potion and began to smear it on himself . . . Luc couldn't see his face although his presence filled the room as if midnight had come and caught him unawares.

Luc felt numb with terror. He breathed heavily. He felt

131

hot, dizzy. He could hear the river of blood ebbing relentlessly through his veins.

Then the figure turned its phantom face towards him and Luc knew him at last. George Gandillon, Pierre's werewolf son, stared at him through the scarlet mists of time . . . He held the bowl out, pointing it towards Luc like the barrel of a gun.

'*Ici, mon frère, pour vous.*'

Luc's hands shot out in front of him. He looked down in horror at the hairs that grew on the back.

'No!' he screamed. He covered his face with his fingers. When he looked up, the image had gone.

Beside him, Jess sprang to her feet.

'Luc . . . what is it? What's wrong?'

He clambered to his feet, held on to her, sobbing.

'By the window . . . it was George Gandillon . . . '

Jess drew his head down to her shoulder. Her hands caressed his hair. 'You must have dozed off, Luc . . . you were dreaming.'

'No, I saw him.'

She held him at a distance. 'Luc, there's nothing there.' She took his hand. 'Come on . . . it must be time.'

He gathered his courage together. 'Yes,' he said. 'It is time.'

There was a lamp burning in the kitchen. An empty brown and cracked jug stood on the table.

'She must have come down for her drink,' Luc said. 'I usually leave it outside her room. She will be asleep by now.'

He lit another lamp and held it up high. He stretched out his hand. 'Come, my Jess.'

He gripped her fingers tightly. Even if she had wanted to run, she could not have escaped.

Along the corridor, the eyes of the family Gandillon followed them to the foot of the dark-shadowed stairway.

Luc's hand holding the lamp trembled with anticipation. The flickering light threw giant shadows into the stairwell.

Silently, they began the long climb upwards. Luc went first, holding the lamp up. On the first landing, he stopped and put his arm about Jess's shoulders. He felt her shaking, but whether it was with cold or fear, he did not know.

He bent to kiss her forehead then wordlessly took her hand and walked on up the second stairway to his mother's room.

He stepped on to the landing and held his finger to his lips. He went to her door and put his ear against the wooden panel.

'It is all right,' he whispered. 'I can hear she sleeps.' He lifted the lamp glass and blew out the light.

'Luc . . . ' Jess hissed behind him. 'I can't see a thing.'

'When we get inside, I will pull back the curtains. A little moonlight is all you need.'

He placed his hand on the door knob and turned it slowly. He pushed it open a crack then listened again.

'Luc . . . ' Jess was growing impatient. Anxious, he knew, to get the task over and done with.

He stepped over the threshold, motioning Jess to follow.

On the floor, amongst the other debris, was a pile of black clothes. The tattered skirt, the scarf his mother wore to cover herself. Jess's hand sought and clutched his. He swallowed the tide of panic that threatened to overcome him. He took a deep breath.

There was a terrible smell in the room . . . of pungent herbs and stuffy air. Beside him, Jess swayed as if she felt dizzy. He heard her take a deep breath as if she was summoning courage that threatened to fail. Luc squeezed her hand, let it fall, then tip-toed over to the window. He drew back one curtain. Moonlight flooded in. It lay across the bed like a silver spear.

Jess was standing, looking at the huddled lump under the clothes. The great, wolfskin cover was drawn up over his mother's head.

'Now, Jess,' he whispered. 'Now.'

Jess seemed hardly aware of what she was doing. As if the room's fetid atmosphere was suffocating her. She bent to move carefully a glass of dark liquid that sat on the bedside table amongst a multitude of other glasses and jars. His nostrils caught a whiff of the pungent and bitter brew. Jess carefully laid the locket down.

Suddenly, Luc's mother moaned and stirred beneath the wolfskin cover. His breath hissed through his teeth. He wondered if Jess realized he was as scared as she.

Jess leaned forward and carefully snapped open the locket.

Three drops for her . . .

She dipped her index finger carefully inside, then, with her other hand, reached out to draw back the cover gently . . .

'Oh . . . my God!' Jess's stifled scream echoed round the room. Her hand flew to her mouth, her eyes wide with horror and disbelief. The locket went spinning away across the mouldering carpet. The glass fell to the floor with a thud.

In one bound, Luc was beside her, his grip hurting her arm.

'Jess . . . !'

Then he looked down too, and it seemed all the breath disappeared from his body. He froze. Then a deep cry came from his throat.

'*Maman!*' His voice was full of confusion and terror. '*Maman . . . !*'

At his cry, his mother's reddened eyelids flew open. She stared at them both for one petrified moment in time. Then she screamed, her maimed and ulcerated hands flying upwards in a desperate attempt to cover her face. But it was too late . . . they had both seen her. The hideously discoloured and disfigured skin, the nose, almost eaten away by some terrible creeping affliction, the patches of long hair growing on her cheeks, the livid lips drawn back over reddish-brown teeth . . . The only part that remained of the once-beautiful face in the portrait downstairs was the long, shiningly abundant black hair. Only now, a stark white streak ran backwards from the ruined temple.

Jess's hand flew to her mouth. Her eyes were wide with horror. 'Oh, my God . . . !'

She gave Luc one fleeting appalled glance, then turned and fled from the room. He heard her boots clattering, flying down the stairs. He plunged after her, calling her name, but she was deaf and blind . . . he knew all she could see and hear was the sight of his mother's terrible face and the screaming, desperate cry as she begged them to leave.

He reached the bottom of the stairs, flying in the wake of Jess's tears. At the kitchen threshold he almost caught her, then suddenly he heard someone call her name. 'Jess!'

. . . And standing in the kitchen was Peggy with her arms outstretched. Luc was dimly aware of two other figures in the room as he saw Jess fall into her aunt's arms and hold on as if her life depended on it.

Luc skidded to a halt in the doorway. Then, with a wild cry, he turned and fled back the way he had come.

Behind, he heard Jess cry. 'Quick . . . we mustn't let him go.'

At the end of the hallway, he tried to wrench open the window. At last, in desperation, he thrust his hand through the glass. It shattered around him. Blood spurted in a scarlet shower. Clutching his punctured arm to his chest, he turned to give one last desperate look at Jess, plunged through the jagged hole and disappeared swiftly into the waiting, moonlit night.

135

1 1

JESS

Jess sat in the waiting-room of the accident and emergency department of the local hospital. Her hands were clutched round a polystyrene cup of tea. She stared at the floor. Beside her, Peggy was speaking to Jack in hushed tones.

In one of the cubicles, Jess could hear a nurse talking quietly to Luc as he stitched and dressed the deep wound in Luc's arm. She bit her thumbnail nervously.

She felt Peggy touch her arm. 'He won't be long now, I shouldn't think.'

Jess gave her a wan smile. 'Hope not.'

'Are you all right, Jess?' Jack asked, leaning forward, his elbows on his knees.

'I'm fine . . . really. I just wish I knew what was going on, that's all.'

It wasn't really true. Jess felt exhausted . . . drained. All she wanted to do was go back to Peggy's, curl up in bed and sleep for a week.

'When Luc comes out, we'll go and find Doctor Prentiss,' Peggy said. 'She'll tell us what's happening, I'm sure.'

Just then, Doctor Prentiss walked through into the casualty department. She came to sit beside them, trying to brush mud from her trousers where she had clambered over the wall at Spital House.

'How is she?' Jess asked anxiously.

The doctor ran her hands through her hair and pulled a face.

'As well as can be expected, I suppose . . . considering how long she's been ill.'

'What is it?' Jess asked. She felt her throat constrict . . . if she wasn't careful she'd start to cry again. 'What's *wrong* with her?'

'As far as we can tell,' the doctor said gently, 'she's suffering from a disease called porphyria . . .'

'What on earth's that?'

'Well . . . it's complicated . . . but basically it's an allergy to sunlight.'

Jess covered her face with her hands. 'Oh, God . . . poor woman.'

'She's been so long without help I'm afraid she's in a terrible state,' the doctor went on. 'They're doing what they can to make her comfortable.'

Jess shook her head. 'I don't understand,' she said. 'According to Luc she never goes out in the sun . . . he said she goes out at night . . . although I did see her in the forest once but she had her face covered up.'

'Yes. We need to talk to Luc, of course, but they think she developed the disease years ago and the lesions on her face have never healed. She has managed to tell us she has been treating herself with herbal remedies although she had no idea what had caused the injuries in the first place. I'm afraid the stuff she's been using has only made the situation worse.'

'But what about that hair . . . ' Jess began.

'It's one of the symptoms, as are the discoloured teeth and ulcerated hands . . . it's a terrible disease and there's no cure I'm afraid, although there are some drugs that may help a little.'

Jess turned to Peggy. 'Oh, Peggy, what are we going to do?'

Peggy put her arm round Jess's shoulders. 'Don't worry, Jess, we'll sort something out. At least she's getting some help now . . . and Luc.'

Jess wiped her eyes. 'Poor Luc.'

'Well, I'm off,' Doctor Prentiss said. 'I'll come up to Peggy's tomorrow to see Luc . . . I assume you are taking him home with you?'

'Yes, of course,' Peggy said. 'Thanks, doctor . . . I'm sorry to have called you so late in the evening . . . I was so worried.'

The doctor smiled wearily. 'No problem.'

Jack went with her to the door.

'Jess . . . ' Peggy began, 'I know we've got to talk things over with Luc when we get back but there is something I want to tell you before he comes out.'

'What?'

Peggy fumbled in her pocket and took out a piece of dried-up red and white fungus. 'When you and Jack ran out to find Luc, I came across this in the kitchen.'

Jess took it from Peggy's hand. She turned it over in her palm, then sniffed it. 'What is it?'

'Well, I'm not absolutely certain but I think it's fly agaric.'

'Fly what?'

'Fly agaric . . . it grows in the forest. It's sometimes called magic mushroom.'

Jess frowned. 'I've read something about that. It's poisonous, isn't it?'

'Yes, very. But eaten in small quantities it causes you to have hallucinations . . . as well as other things.'

Jess looked at her in horror. 'Do you mean Luc and his mother have been eating it?'

Peggy raised her eyebrows. 'It looks like it. In its early stage of growth it can easily be mistaken for another mushroom that's completely harmless. They've obviously only had small quantities otherwise it would have killed them.'

Jess put her head in her hands. 'Oh, God, Peggy . . . what a mess. No wonder poor Luc thought his mother was . . . '

'What?'

She looked at Peggy. What was the point of telling her? It was over . . . finished. Her stomach tightened. She would never forget the sight of Luc's mother's ruined face. The sound of her despairing voice, begging them to leave, would

be with Jess for ever. But it was time to look forward . . .
not back. If there was one thing Danny's betrayal had
taught her—it was that.

'Oh . . . nothing,' she said.

Peggy looked at her shrewdly but said no more.

Just then, the curtains in one of the cubicles were drawn
back. Jess saw the nurse come out with a pale-looking Luc.
His arm was bandaged and in a sling. The lumberjack's coat
was draped around his naked shoulders. She saw his eyes
searching for her and when they finally rested on her face
he gave her a small, sad smile.

She ran towards him and took his hand.

'Come on, Luc,' she said. 'Let's go home.'

Back at Peggy's, the fire was out and the kitchen grown cold.
They sat Luc by the hearth while Peggy bustled about
getting the stove going. Jess made a hot drink and brought it
to him. He thanked her with a smile and sat staring silently
into the flames, his hands clasped round the warmth of the
mug.

Jess sat on the floor beside him.

'What are you going to do now, Luc?' She gazed up at
him, waiting for his answer.

Luc shrugged. 'I do not know . . . wait for my mother to
come home, I suppose.'

'Luc, she could be in hospital for ages, you can't stay in
that place by yourself.'

'You can stay here,' Peggy said. 'There's plenty of room
and I need someone to help with the animals.'

But he looked unsure.

Jess took his cold hand into her own. 'It'll give you time
to decide what to do,' she said. 'To think about your
future.'

He gazed at her. 'Yes,' he said. 'But you, Jess, you will
not be here.'

Jess lowered her eyes. She would like nothing better than

139

to stay here too. But she knew it was impossible. She *had* to go back. She had to sort things out with her parents. She had to face Charlene, she *had* to get back to normality. Then there was college . . . But the course wouldn't last for ever. When it was finished she would be free to do as she pleased.

'Not for a while,' Jess told him. 'But I'll come back as soon as I can, I promise.'

Luc glanced up at Peggy, standing over them both. Then he looked at Jess, raised the back of her hand to his lips and kissed it gently.

'Very well,' he said. 'I will wait.'

EPILOGUE

Excerpt from the Forest Weekly News—*16 January.*

'BEAST MYSTERY SOLVED'

Forest beast caught at last

Farmers and smallholders breathed a sigh of relief this week when the animal dubbed locally as *the forest beast* was tracked down and shot.

Local RSPCA officers and veterinary surgeon Jack Stride have been trying to track the animal down for some time. It was eventually traced to a hideout in a cave in the forest on Tuesday morning. Mr Stride said, 'The animal, a large dog, is believed to be the offspring of a Canadian timber wolf and a large domestic dog, possibly a mastiff, known to have been at large for several months after escaping from a local kennel last year. The animal had obviously been living in the cave since its mother abandoned it. From evidence found inside, it had been existing on foxes, rabbits, and small mammals until the bad weather drove it nearer to local farms and smallholdings.'

Mr Stride expressed regret at having had to kill the dog. 'We had hoped to capture it alive,' he said. 'But it caught us unawares and we had to shoot it.'

PORPHYRIA

In porphyria there is some disturbance of the metabolism and this results in a variegated picture which includes discolouration of the urine, skin rashes due to sensitization of the skin to light, various forms of indigestion and mental disturbances.

Blacks Medical Dictionary (37th edition, 1992)

CONGENITAL ERYTHROPOIETIC PORPHYRIA

This disease is characterized by red discolouration of urine and teeth, excessive hair growth, severe skin blistering and ulceration and haemolytic anaemia.

The B.M.A. Family Health Encyclopaedia (Dorling Kindersley)

FLY AGARIC (*Amanita Muscaria*)

Perhaps the best known poisonous mushroom depicted by illustrators to conjure up the mysterious world of toadstools. Its toxins will attack the nervous system producing such effects as auditory and visual hallucination, euphoria, hyperactivity, and irregular heartbeat.